"You'd anyth

He shook her. "Wouldn't you?"

"Yes!" Zoe screamed at him, driven beyond caring by the foul things he implied. "Yes, I'd do anything because I love you. But I've only gone to bed with one man—you, Ross." A sob broke her voice. "If you were to ask me, I'd never make love from this moment on to prove how much I love you, because sex without love is meaningless to me."

His lip curled. "There's no need for such a sacrifice," he mocked, turning away. "There are plenty of wealthy men who'd be pleased to avail themselves of your charms—for a price. But not me. Never again me."

Her heart ached for what might have been. They were two lost souls on the way to a hell of their own devising....

AMANDA BROWNING is a new British author who lives in Essex. She is single, and a former librarian. We believe the lively contemporary writing style of her first book, *Perfect Strangers*, will appeal to readers everywhere.

AMANDA BROWNING

perfect strangers

Harlequin Books

TORONTO • NEW YORK • LONDON
AMSTERDAM • PARIS • SYDNEY • HAMBURG
STOCKHOLM • ATHENS • TOKYO • MILAN

Harlequin Presents first edition March 1988
ISBN 0-373-11055-3

Original hardcover edition published in 1987
by Mills & Boon Limited

CHAPTER ONE

HE was lying on one of the hotel's white, wooden-slatted sun loungers beneath a shady beach umbrella when Zoe emerged from the cooling warmth of the blue-green sea. She didn't see him immediately, for water still trickled into her eyes, but then she became aware of the relaxed, tanned figure, and it seemed for a moment that her heart stood still, and then accelerated rapidly until her whole body shook with it. The slight rise of the pale sand rocked as the shockwave ran through her. She had known he was coming, but not that it would be today. She wasn't prepared.

Every fibre of her being recognised him—awakening from a long sleep. Ross Lyneham, the owner of the island, creator of the hotel complex . . . and the man she had come to find.

Yet once the first shock had subsided she was left wondering what to do. Her first blind instinct to confront him had to be ruthlessly curbed, for to do anything precipitate might well ruin her chances before ever they had the opportunity to succeed. She chewed her lip. Need that deny her the pleasure of taking a closer look as he slept? Looking couldn't hurt him, and it would help her.

Half a dozen steps brought her to the side of the lounger, her approach muffled by the soft sand. She could hear her own slightly ragged breathing quite loudly over the constant wash of the waves, and expected that at any moment he would hear it too and open his eyes. But the even rise and fall of his chest did not falter.

His head was angled towards her, and here there were still signs of a recent ordeal in skin drawn too tightly over high cheekbones. Faint lines studded his forehead, and still others slanted down to where his naturally full lips were thinned into a firm line from hours of pain. She couldn't see his eyes, for the lids, with their long, thick lashes, shielded them from her view. One lock of hair fell across his forehead and drew her eyes inevitably upwards to where the thick waves were tousled into a halo of brown laced with gold. It lay lush at his nape, a rich golden honey-brown, warm and inviting her to touch.

She moved, her action instinctive and unplanned, and as she did so, the femininely thick-lashed lids opened and she was speared on the end of a sea-green gaze. Caught, immobile, with her hand stretched out towards him. A wave of heat rose into her cheeks as she realised how brazen her stance must seem. She waited, scarcely breathing. What would he do? Would the shock . . .? What he did was raise one straight eyebrow to enquire wordlessly, with a quirk of his lips, just what she thought she was doing.

Then, almost as if he had been aware of her hungry inspection, his gaze roved over her in its turn. Her skimpy bikini was unhurriedly stripped away beneath that scalding scrutiny, and the audacious gleam in the eyes he eventually returned to her flushed face told her he liked what his imagination had uncovered. His boldness took her breath away.

'Hello.' That one word, uttered in a rich, deep rumble, conveyed a thousand different nuances to set her pulse racing chaotically. 'Are you going to tell me who you are?'

It didn't seem possible that so simple a question could deal the harshest blow, yet it did, and with the need to remain unmoved never more necessary, she dug her nails into her palms to hold back her sense of betrayal. Hastily lowered lids hid her pain, then lifted again. 'I'm Zoe Winthrop, Mr Lyneham. Welcome back to Mariposa,' she forced out, surprising herself at how cool she sounded.

With a sinking heart she watched his brows rise and his eyes take on a knowing gleam as once more they strayed from her face down the enticement of her still wet body and up again. Slowly he smiled and tipped his head to view her flushed face. The hand he raised to clasp hers was firm and strong, but as he let hers go again he quite deliberately trailed his fingers over her palm.

Even in shock it was enough to send an electrical charge up her arm, and Zoe struggled to hide her body's instinctive reaction to the sexual tease. Unsuccessfully. Ross Lyneham's attention returned to the proud thrust of her breasts against the confining material of her bikini top. When at last he spoke, his tone was distinctly mocking.

'That's very kind of you, Zoe Winthrop. If I'd known such a delectable welcome was awaiting me, I'd have come sooner. I take it you work at the hotel. Mike's taste is improving.'

It shook her to realise he thought she was issuing a come-on, but not as much as the blatant way he responded to it. She gasped out an unsteady, 'I didn't... I wouldn't...'

He regarded her disbelievingly from beneath sleepy lids and laughed. 'Honey, it doesn't matter if you didn't or wouldn't—you have. You get full marks for a novel approach, but as you can see, I'm too bushed to follow it up right now. Keep it warm for me, hmn? My appetite will be all the keener later on.'

She wasn't stupid enough to believe food had any

relevance to his words, but in her stunned condition she didn't take offence. No, it was the manner, not the content of his reply that had her trembling inside. Her heart began to thud apprehensively. She had never expected to feel so out of her depth.

Watching her expression change, the man on the lounger began to laugh. 'Why bother to pretend, honey? You're beautiful, you have a very sexy body, both of which interest me greatly. But you knew that before you *chassé'd* over here. Oh, I'm not turning you down. What man would refuse an alluring package like you? Let's just say I'm savouring the moment.'

Zoe felt the hot wash of colour come and go in her cheeks and was choked. She forced herself to utter a denial, but it hurt to have to do it.

'I didn't intend what you so obviously imagine when I came over here.' How she wished now she hadn't given in to the impulse, but it had been too strong—always would be. Only . . . this wasn't how it was supposed to be.

Openly mocking now, he shook his head slightly. 'OK, honey. Let's pretend you weren't shooting me a line, you just came over to say hello. I'm happy to take things slower if my haste affronts you.' All too clearly to Zoe he didn't believe a word of it, but was humouring her. 'So, tell me, what do you do here?'

Tensely aware of the vast hollow inside her, she welcomed the shift to solid ground. 'I sing, in the . . .' The sudden tensing of his whole body and the starkly angry glitter that totally wiped away the mocking appreciation of her from his eyes had her stumbling to a halt. His face was twisted into an alien mask that jolted her nerves and made her think she was about to be violently ill.

'So, you're a singer?' His hostility was sickening.

Zoe forced down the nausea to say, 'You make it

sound as if you have something against singers.' Lord, she just wanted to run away and cry at his expression.

His laugh was humourlessly self-mocking. 'Do I have something against singers?' he jeered, and laughed again, until she wanted to scream at him to shut up. 'You could say that. Oh, yes, you could definitely say that!' he drawled harshly. His green gaze burnt her like ice. 'And how much is Mike paying you to . . . sing? At a guess I'd say you don't come cheap.'

Anger at the slur overcame shock. 'I'm paid what I'm worth, Mr Lyneham, no more. I suggest you discuss it with Mike after you've heard me sing.'

'Oh, I will, sweetheart.' He took her up on it, 'Where business is concerned everyone pulls their weight or they're out. I might find you desirable, but no woman, whatever her talents, gets by on looks alone in my company.'

Lost as she was in the morass of his disgust, Zoe's chin still went up. 'I've never traded on my looks!' she fired back angrily.

'I've never known a beautiful singer not to.' His retort cut like a knife.

Her eyes widened in amazement at the sheer unfairness of that. 'Then you haven't known many,' she defended, so disturbed that her response was automatic.

As she watched, his expression became bleak. 'One too many, sweetheart. Just one too many.' For a moment Zoe saw he wasn't even with her, his thoughts were far away and far from pleasant. Then, with a visible shake of his head, he came back to her. His inspection was outrageous. 'On the other hand, forewarned is forearmed, as they say. With the right inducement I could overlook the drawback. You are a very delectable woman. Once I get over the jet-lag I have no doubt I'll sup at your feast and be replete.'

The change from icy distaste to sexual innuendo made Zoe reel. Reaction made her tremble, only her legs were so weak she couldn't move away as every protective instinct she possessed was urging her to do. Not like this, she wanted to tell him, please, not like this. But in the face of the stranger he was, she couldn't. Yet despite everything she was unwilling to leave him so soon, because she could see fatigue blurring the handsome lines of his face. Concern overcame her distress at his continued insistence that her designs were totally mercenary.

Composure now was paramount, but the effort to achieve it was exhausting. 'I . . . we, all heard about your accident. Are you quite well now?' She managed to hide her anxiety, though she watched every changing expression on his face intently.

'Oh, I'm just great. Fit as a fiddle,' he jeered caustically. 'If the headaches don't kill me, the frustration will!'

Because she had expected nothing more than a polite reply, Zoe was astounded. There was no mistaking the frustration he claimed, his disgusted voice was full of it. She swept from shock to shock like a piece of flotsam.

'Meaning?' she prompted, stilling an urge to demand what he meant by saying the headaches would kill him. Panic would serve no useful purpose. She had to keep going.

Exasperation was the prime motivator in the glance he shot her. 'Certain people who should damn well know better insist on molly-coddling me as if I were an invalid. Pretty soon one of them is going to do it once too often and end up with a black eye for his trouble.'

Whoever he was referring to, they had her sympathy. 'Perhaps they've been told to do it. Doctor's orders,' she offered in mitigation, even as she felt for him. Enforced idleness would go very much against the grain. He wasn't a workaholic, but he ran it a close second.

'Of course they have,' he barked testily, 'but if anyone knows if I'm fit to work, then I'm that person, not some quack or other!'

Biting back the need to tell him not to bark at her, Zoe tempered, 'Then how do you feel?'

'Wondering if I'm fit enough to keep up with you?' he mocked.

Her sense of violation sent her rigid, so that for a moment all she could do was stare at him and try to swallow. That her concern should be so misunderstood! 'I'm sorry, obviously I'm being a nuisance.'

His hand on her wrist stopped her movement away from him. 'Don't go cold on me, honey. You just chose a sore subject.'

She couldn't argue with that. She could understand it. It was the rest that dismayed her. She had walked up to him with the simple intention of satisfying herself that he was well—and had stepped into an emotional nightmare.

Fighting in the dark, she licked her lips. 'Perhaps you should slow down.'

'I've got too much on to rest as they want me to do,' he argued.

Anyone who knew him was aware of his great drive in all his undertakings, especially business. The slightest disability would be anathema to him. His brain would detest the knowledge that his body couldn't keep up his usual rugged pace. The trouble was, he would keep testing himself, pushing himself to the limit, determined to prove that he could cope, getting more and more frustrated every time it was proved that he couldn't. He'd hate himself.

Knowing that, Zoe still attempted to offer advice. 'If

you rested more now, you'd get better quicker.'

She had said the wrong thing again, and he positively glowered at her. 'And what would you know about it? Have you ever spent months in a hospital bed, then weeks feeling so weak even a baby could do more?'

Her stomach lurched. She could have told him, could have said so much, but he didn't want to hear her understand. He sounded as if he were spoiling for an argument. The argument everyone close to him was probably at pains to stop him from indulging in. Zoe was inclined to think he would be better off getting it all out of his system. On the other hand, she was in no state herself to weather the storm. Every word he uttered buffeted her emotions until she didn't know if she were on her head or her heels. She felt like a ghost and knew she must look it.

Once again Ross exhibited that lightning change of mood. 'You're going to tell me I shouldn't be taking my bad humour out on you, and you're right. There are other things I'd rather do with you than argue. In fact, I could be persuaded to go to bed—with the incentive of the right companion.'

Zoe's heart rate, which had been fluctuating alarmingly during their exchanges, increased and she flushed angrily, reaching the limits of her control. 'I don't know why you should keep insulting me, Mr Lyneham, by assuming I can't wait to jump into bed with you. I'm not the type you think I am.'

'Are you not?' he asked without much interest in her denial. 'Well, perhaps you're right about me. I haven't always known the right type of woman. Meet me for lunch tomorrow, say one o'clock, and I'll give you a chance to prove you're different.'

Such an opportunity shouldn't have been necessary, and surely, to prove herself different, she should refuse,

not accept, but she couldn't bring herself to do it. Even
faced with the lack of respect he showed her. Yet it
wasn't that simple.

'I'd like that, but I don't usually wake up till the
afternoon.' She was given no chance to explain the
statement further.

Ross shrugged, 'Fair enough, honey, I can easily find
another companion.'

He couldn't have made it plainer that he wasn't
worried if he saw her again or not, and it cut like a blunt
knife. 'Oh, but . . .'

He studied her with a knowing look. 'Honey, if you
want to join me you'll make time. If not, forget it. Look
me up when you've made up your mind. On an island
this size, I won't be far away.' As far as he was
concerned, the ball was in her court. She could either
return it or let it pass.

Caught by the maelstrom of emotions inside her, Zoe
could do neither. Everything she had locked out came
crowding back, buffeting and bruising. Her protective
coating could no longer withstand the assault on her
vulnerability. She could never have been prepared for
the man she had met today.

She began to excuse herself. 'I won't disturb you any
longer then.'

Tired he might be, but his eyes had no trouble
following the nervy movement of her hand against her
thigh, and he found her words extremely amusing. 'You
have to be kidding me, honey,' he jeered, closing his eyes
on a laugh.

His lips twitched as she gasped, and with her insides
churning, Zoe hesitated for only a moment before
hurrying away on legs that quaked at the knees. At the
band of trees which curtained off the hotel complex
from the beach, she halted and glanced back. The tanned

figure hadn't moved, and neither could she.

Zoe stared at him and felt the strength which had seen her through the last few minutes drain out of her limbs. A fine trembling forced her to hold on to the solid bulk of the tree beside her. Her brain, independent of her emotions, had carried her through when the first glance from green eyes had spelled out the death of her hopes.

He had not recognised her.

Ross Lyneham—the man she loved, the man she had been going to marry—did not know her.

Only then did she feel the deep cut of pain that his closeness had kept at bay. It lanced through her, twisting her face into a broken mask of despair. The sudden death of hope was agonising. She had thought that if he only could see her, then he would remember, but he had acted as if she were no more important to him than the countless other women who swam in and out of his life.

Zoe couldn't bear to look at him, turning away to lean her back against the tree, her arms crossed protectively about her waist. Her heart had been wrenched from her, and the torture of watching it die before her eyes forced a moan from her tight-drawn throat.

No good telling herself she had been warned, she had had to find out for herself and the truth was almost more than she could bear. Eight months she had waited for him to get well and send for her, getting by with the loving support of her family. The accident that had swept them apart had now added another casualty to the list: his love for her was dead. So far as he knew, it had never existed, while Zoe was left loving him and knowing he could pass her by and not feel any loss.

It was the picture of him in the papers, a beautiful blonde attached to his arm, which had spurred her on to seek him out against all the advice. Her parents were concerned for her. She had had to tell them what she intended to do, and they had tried to talk her out of it, but she had refused to be swayed from her decision. In the end they had been forced to let her go. They couldn't have stopped her, but they had made her promise to keep in touch, because if she didn't they would simply follow her out there to check for themselves. There had been a lot of tears, but their love and worry had been obvious. She didn't want to hurt them, but she had had to put an end to the waiting. Yet she had been careful because she had known she couldn't just turn up in New York, where he lived. Painful memories warned her that she must have some protection. So she had used her talent as a professional singer to win a spot in the nightclub on Mariposa, knowing that Ross was bound to come. He visited all his businesses regularly—so it was only a matter of time.

She had been content to wait because she had been so certain he would remember her. How wrong she was. How bitter the result.

The piercing call of a bird in the tree above awakened her to the vulnerability of her position. She couldn't let Ross find her here. She couldn't face him again with any composure until she had herself under control again. Until she had decided what to do.

It was a relief to return to her small chalet and lean back on the door as it closed behind her. The hands she raised to smooth over her hair were far from steady, but the air-conditioning began to work its soothing caress on her overheated flesh.

Her attention was caught by her reflection in the full-length mirror of her wardrobe. The sight that met her eyes brought her no ease. Her face had no colour and her golden eyes were large and full of stark pain. Her skin felt tight with strain over her cheeks and her lips had lost their sensual fullness in her attempt to still their trembling. Her eyes sought their reflection. What was she going to do? Why couldn't she have made him remember he loved her? Once it had been so perfect. A shudder of remembrance ran through her. Precisely how the notion took form she didn't know, but the force of its promise made her gasp. He had loved her once—couldn't he do so again? Surely there was more than a slim chance that it could happen? All she had to do was act the stranger he thought she was and let love grow as it had before.

But the odds were different now, a small voice warned. How can you make a man love you with two such black marks against you—your looks and your profession? Ross had always been attracted to beautiful women, but he had never behaved to them as he had to her today. And what about his attitude to her profession? He had sounded as if he actually detested it, yet he had always had the utmost appreciation of such talented people before.

She couldn't understand it. It didn't fit in with what she knew of him. He had sounded so hard and cynical, so disbelieving that there could be any goodness in her because of what she did. What had happened to make him think this way? How could she prove to him it simply wasn't true? She just didn't know, but she would have to find a way. She loved him, she wasn't giving up because the first fence was so difficult. His attitude made her cringe, but she would put up with his innuendoes if it gave her the chance to get close and prove just how wrong he was. It wouldn't be easy, but then nothing worthwhile ever was. Only she would know if it failed. Only she would be hurt beyond bearing. Yet it was better to try and to fail than not to try at all.

Hope lightened the gold in her eyes to a bright glitter. God, how good it felt to have some purpose, some goal, where only moments ago she had been cut to the bone.

Now she studied herself critically. Her fair hair was salt-caked, but a shower would soon return it to its blonde glory. Her body's reflection always came as a shock. She could never be described as dainty, for she stood five feet seven in her stockinged feet, but she wasn't built on a grand scale. That was why she had always found the fulness of her breasts and the rich curve of hip and thigh something of an embarrassment. Yet Ross had always liked to look at her, and touch her. That was a good thing to remember. A positive thing.

Instinct told her that in the days to come she would need to cling to her good memories in order to weather the inexplicable changes in Ross. It would be her only defence, her love for him her only weapon.

And if it all became too much, there was always her singing. That was the cause of the odd lifestyle Ross hadn't understood. The nightclub was open from ten o'clock at night till four in the morning and she and another singer, Marian Ritchie, split the shift. It meant they were nearly always asleep when the rest of the island was just getting into the day, but she didn't mind. She enjoyed the cosy atmosphere of the club in the night hours, fingers crossing the ivory keys of the piano while her husky voice easily poured out the blues or jazz numbers she adored, and the romantic ballads that were always popular with the guests.

In her singing she could express emotions that came from deep within, and as she went to shower off the salt and sand, she found herself humming 'Plaisir d'Amour'. The words said the joy of love only lasted a moment, that the pain endured a lifetime. Well, she had suffered enough for two lifetimes, surely soon she must experience some of the joy. It was the hope that kept her going.

Since coming to the island, she had always included

one song every night that was for Ross, even though he wasn't there. That evening it was different, because no longer were they oceans apart, but only the width of a room. She heard the buzz that went round the club shortly before she picked him out for herself. He had always commanded attention. From men because they admired him, and from women because they wanted him. Tonight was no different. Zoe watched him too, pride at his virile appearance warring with dismay at the newly acquired cynicism with which he reviewed the latter.

She was conscious of him every second until he left an hour later. Had it really been a coincidence that he departed immediately after she sang the lines about reading her mind and discovering what a fascinating tale it told?

He had made no attempt to acknowledge their earlier meeting, but he had watched her. There could be no mistake. His eyes had seemed to be on her every time she looked in his direction, which she found herself doing frequently for he exerted a powerful magnetic force. If only she could be sure he was watching her with interest, not scorn. That had tempted her. It was always the same. When something troubled her, she expressed herself in song. She sighed softly. It was something Ross didn't know for he had never heard her sing this way. They hadn't been together long enough for him to discover it.

Which was why his departure had everything to do with the words that next came to her lips, a haunting melody that said all she couldn't say—that he was her bright sun, without him she lived in a perpetual winter. It took a determined effort to block him from her mind after that, for his going had left a void that only his vital presence could refill.

She didn't sleep well that night. Memories came back

to haunt her, bringing with them all the anguish she had known as if it were yesterday. They had been so happy, so sure of the future and what it held for them. Nothing could ever keep them apart. Nothing—except cruel fate, and a vindictiveness that life had not prepared her for.

Daylight helped her repair the chinks in her defences. After breakfast Zoe made her way to the office to see Mike Farrell, the manager. Some of the notes she had played last night had sounded off, and she wanted to arrange for a tuner to be flown over. She was surprised to find the door closed, but her knock received a reply, so she went in. Only it wasn't the cheery figure, with the thinning fair hair, of the manager who sat behind the desk, but Ross. He was listening on the end of the telephone, and whatever was being said didn't meet with his approval, for his face was thunderous. He waved her in, then turned his attention back to his caller.

'I may have lost some weeks of my life, Hal, but not my mind. What you're telling me is a load of bull and you know it. Kindly get me the information I asked for. I'll hold.' He transferred his scowl to Zoe. 'Were you looking for me?'

Not in this mood, she said to herself, before answering. 'Actually, no. I wanted to see Mike about something.'

A rueful smile altered his face completely and he ran a distracted hand through his hair. 'That's a pity, I could use some light entertainment.'

The sight of his smile had winded her and she gathered her scattered wits hastily. 'Sorry, but I don't do private shows for jaded businessmen,' she quipped.

Ross laughed, but it was half-hearted. 'What about forgetful ones?'

Did that mean she had jogged his memory after all? Zoe's heart skipped a beat and she forced herself to be cautious. 'I . . . don't understand.'

'Naturally not,' he agreed drily. 'I've just been reminded that the project I'm working on is something I covered before the crash, and I don't recall any of it. If I hear one more sympathetic voice telling me not to worry, heads will roll.'

Her disappointment was deep, but so was her concern for him. At the moment it didn't matter that he had turned into this cynical man. He was hurting from his loss of memory even as she was, yet she couldn't ease his mind as she wanted to.

'I can't imagine what it's like, but it must be frustrating,' she offered lightly, not wanting to draw his anger by being too sympathetic herself.

'A totally inadequate word, I've discovered,' he drawled scathingly, and it was as if her words had opened a safety valve. 'You wake up each morning thinking perhaps today will be the day something goes click in your brain and everything will fall into place. Each night you tell yourself, what the heck, maybe tomorrow. And it goes on and on. You feel like committing murder because nothing and nobody helps your recall, and that's when it hits you. What if you did murder someone, and that's why you can't remember.'

Zoe watched in acute distress as the accumulated anger of impotence spewed out. She hadn't thought, had never imagined he would feel like this, and she was standing here knowing everything yet unable to say a word to help him.

'But didn't the doctors say it was the accident?' she interjected unhappily.

That drew a rapier look. 'Surely even you know that most cases of amnesia are caused by the wish to forget something unpalatable.'

'Not always, though.'

'In my case I suspect it happens to be true. Oh, not murder, but something,' His eyes held hers. For a moment she thought he had finished, but then he went on as if he couldn't help himself. 'Do you know, it wasn't until some weeks after I came out of the coma that I found out I didn't remember everything. Can you even begin to conceive how unnerving it is to be asked a question that leaves your mind a total blank? You know those cartoons where someone runs off the cliff and doesn't realise for a moment that there is nothing solid beneath his feet, then he plummets into the void? That was exactly how I felt when they asked me about . . .' He stopped and grimaced at the interrupted thought.

Zoe wanted quite desperately to go to him and tell him there was nothing for him to be fearful of discovering, quite the contrary, only it wasn't possible. Already he had papered over the crack that betrayed his vulnerability, and there was no way through for her.

'You have managed to piece some things together, though?' she asked instead, hating the role she was being forced to play.

He looked disgusted. 'Sure, piece is the appropriate word. Apparently the way to do it is find out for yourself, hoping something will click. Amnesiacs are supposed to be wet-nursed against emotional damage. Nothing is said about how you feel when you find yourself in the dark like this.'

'Nothing happened, then?' she probed carefully.

'With a lot of detective work I found out the basic details, and going over things I can generally come to the same conclusions as I did before when it comes to my business. After all, nothing has changed much there. What I want to know is what the hell happened to me personally in those weeks that makes me need to forget!'

This was uncharted territory, and Zoe licked her lips.

'Don't you think it's more likely nothing did, that you're simply blowing it all up in your mind with trying too hard?' she ventured.

His look was quelling. 'Now you sound like my doctor.'

'He must know what he's talking about,' she suggested.

His agreement was sarcastic. 'Naturally, but he knows how difficult it is to stop thinking.'

'Then what did he suggest you do?'

Reluctant amusement softened the grim lines of his face. 'Take a holiday and forget all about it. During which I make a simple phone call and wham, something else I've forgotten surfaces. It twists the gut until you can't think straight. If people knew how unacceptable not being able to remember is, they wouldn't so happily long to forget. I have answers to which I don't know the questions, and questions I don't know who to ask, or where to go to ask. They go round and round inside my head until even I feel like I'm cracking up.'

Her throat was so tight it hurt. 'If there's anything I can do to help.'

The way his eyes shrivelled her made her almost regret the offer. 'I've had more offers of help than I can stomach right now.'

Zoe winced. 'I'm sorry, I just thought . . . well, I know it's about your private life you can't remember, but surely your office could help. A man as important as you would hardly vanish off the face of the earth. If, say, you went abroad, surely someone would know.'

For some reason that made him relax, although from what he said afterwards she didn't know why. 'There you hit a problem, honey. You see, for once in my life I did the unusual, I cut myself off from everything to do with work. The only thing I do know is the very thing I would dearly love to forget.' Before she could dig deeper into that remark, his attention was drawn back to the telephone and for minutes he was busy making notes. At the end his manner was more mollified. 'Thanks, Hal, I'll get back to you in a day or two.' He slapped a folder shut as he replaced the receiver and sank back into his chair. He had undergone another change of humour in the interim, and to her frustration their interrupted conversation was dismissed. Instead he allowed his green gaze to run appreciatively over her attractive figure in its ice-pink sundress. 'So, you didn't come to join me for lunch. I'm desolate.'

She couldn't keep up with his swinging temperament, but she had to follow his lead even though her heart was crying out to know more. She could only hope another chance would come. At least for the moment he sounded teasing and not mocking. She recalled his loving teasing with an aching sense of loss, which made her reply sharper than she had intended. 'You don't look it!'

Ross spread his hands deprecatingly, 'All women like to know they'll be missed,' he stated blandly.

Zoe didn't like being lumped in like that and her indignation showed in the stiffening of her body. 'I'm not all women.'

His lips twitched and his eyes were mockingly sensual. 'No, but definitely all woman.' Which statement, accompanied by his look, made her feel ridiculously breathless again.

'Hell, sometimes you look damn young.' Ross swore angrily when she didn't say anything. 'How old are you anyway?'

'Twenty-three,' she answered, thinking the least he could have done was look her up in the personnel files. At least that would have implied interest.

'Thank God for that! Teenagers and virgins aren't in my line.'

'Implying as I'm not one, I'm therefore not the other,' Zoe snapped, her hand going to her chest because it felt so tight. He hadn't minded that she was a virgin before. In fact he had considered it an honour, and she had been proud to give him the purity of both her body and her love. Now, with careless words, he was subtly destroying her most private memories.

There was a nasty twist to his beautiful mouth. 'I don't know what the equivalent of the casting couch is for singers, but I have little doubt there is one,' Ross stated derisively.

Zoe felt sick. How could he even suggest such a thing? What did he think she was? 'That's a vile thing to say,' she forced out past the agonising lump in her throat. She felt her colour draining away.

Ross was unrepentant. 'I speak as I find. It doesn't put me off indulging in a pleasant romantic interlude with you. In fact, it ensures we'll both get pleasure out of it. How you go about getting to the top of your profession is of little interest to me.'

Oh, God! Zoe closed her eyes to hide her agony. She didn't understand. He'd never say that sort of thing. He'd never go out of his way to be derogatory no matter what he thought. There was something wrong, there had to be. Only she was far too shaken to stay and argue with him. She had to go before he hurt her any more. She forced herself to look at him, unaware that her topaz eyes were clouded with pain.

'Look, I came to ask Mike to have the piano tuned. Would you pass the message on please? I . . . I have some things I must do,' she invented.

Ross nodded, but he was frowning. He even looked a

little uncomfortable. 'What I said ... don't take it personally.'

'Oh?' Zoe's smile was as sardonic as any of his. 'Is there any other way to take it?'

Ross pulled a face. 'It's not my way to condemn out of hand, but there are things you don't know. If I've insulted you, of course I apologise,' he offered, thereby still leaving a margin for doubt. He smiled his charming smile. 'Let's just say I once saw something nasty in the woodshed and never got over it.' He paused for her reaction, which, at the mention of one of their favourite books, brought a reluctant smile to her lips. 'About lunch. We'll make it another time, when I'm in a better mood and not waiting on telephone calls.'

Which at least allowed her to leave with some dignity. Yet the incident preyed on her mind over the next few days. She regained her equilibrium with some effort. Ross didn't know how much his words were hurting her, she couldn't change that. His amnesia had to be lived with. But his general attitude was a complete mystery. Somewhere between his accident and their meeting, something had happened to him, and until she could discover what it was she had to weather his scorn as best she could.

CHAPTER TWO

ZOE didn't see Ross again for two days, then he suddenly appeared as she was practising at the piano. Nothing was going right today. Her voice sounded tired and her head was beginning to pound. Out of sorts with everything, Zoe brought her hands down on the keys with a discordant cacophony that did her nerves and her headache very little good.

That was precisely the moment Ross chose to saunter on to the small stage.

She watched him as he came towards her. He moved with confidently controlled power. Even with his hands tucked casually into the pockets of a pair of baggy white slacks, and his blue short-sleeved shirt left half open to the cool breezes, he looked ruggedly attractive and far, far too vibrantly male. He reacted on that core of sensuality in her as no other man ever had or ever would. It was as natural as breathing.

An art Zoe was finding difficult to control herself. Her mouth all of a sudden felt like the inside of a coal-scuttle, and she swallowed carefully. When he wasn't speaking it was easy to see him as the loving companion he had been to her, but it only served to emphasise how much he had changed.

'Is it you or the piano who's out of tune?' he queried drily.

Zoe laughed. 'I have to admit it's both.'

Ross came to stand beside her, experimenting with a few notes, casually brushing her fingers as he did so. 'Perhaps you should give up and just relax for today.

You can push yourself too far.'

Zoe recovered her fingers as unobtrusively as she could, so that he shouldn't guess at the fierce wave of longing that his touch invoked. 'Setting yourself as a prime example, of course,' she goaded.

Raised eyebrows appreciated her point. '*Et tu*?' he quoted, his eyes dropping to where the fulness of her lips broke into a smile.

Talking helped to cover the tremble of lips his gaze caressed. 'I'm sorry, it just slipped out. But as you can see, I'm as professional about my work as you are about yours. I have to alter my routine every night or people will soon be bored. There again, I'm often asked to sing numbers I haven't sung for some time, and I have to practise them. I can't really afford to take time off and do the songs justice. I won't worry too much now. It will be all right on the night.'

Ross heard her out but made it obvious he was more interested in the way her lips moved than in the words they formed. 'Very commendable. However, even you have to eat. With lunch being out of the question, I've come to suggest you have dinner with me this evening.'

Quickly she lowered her lids to shield her expression. If he saw how eager she was to be with him, there was no saying what his reaction would be. But it seemed she had not been quick enough, for when she looked up again, that hatefully knowing smile lurked in his eyes.

'Don't act coy,' he commanded silkily, 'it's a little late for that. I've already seen that you want to come. You don't have to gain my interest, you've already got it. We're both adults who know the way the game is played. Let's cut out the preamble, shall we? Are you going to join me?'

Patience, it appeared, was no longer his long suit. His abrupt assumption that she would go along with everything he suggested angered her. 'I do have to work tonight,' she retaliated sharply, her attention on the keyboard as she practised a few chords. It was unnerving the way he attracted and repelled her by turns.

Deftly Ross caught one hand, imprisoning it between his own much larger ones. Zoe's eyes shot to his, startled by his action and unsettled by her response to his warm touch. 'Interesting,' he mused as he studied her, 'there's a hint of claws beneath this soft skin.' When, in an effort to pull away, her nails scored his hand, he laughed triumphantly.

Finding he wasn't about to give up her hand, Zoe took a steadying breath, only to lose it again as he moved and his thigh brushed hers. 'I still have to work,' she murmured unsteadily.

Green eyes crinkled up at the corners as he smiled. 'I wasn't suggesting a midnight feast, however tempting the thought turns out to be.'

Feeling more agitated by the minute at this continued closeness, Zoe hastily muttered her agreement. The touch of his hands wasn't enough. The need to be held close in his arms was shocking in its ferocity, and she was desperately afraid that she couldn't hide it from him if he continued to touch her.

Ross finally let her go, his glittering smile telling her he had known all along how vulnerable she was to his touch and had used it against her.

'That's settled then,' he stated unromantically, and Zoe knew that was how he saw it, as a deal successfully completed. He felt inclined to dalliance and she had shown she wasn't averse to the idea. Nothing more than that.

Now Ross settled himself against the piano and crossed his arms. 'I enjoyed your performance the other evening. You're a very talented lady.'

Zoe didn't miss the *double entendre*. 'I didn't think you stayed around long enough to know,' she replied waspishly, then watching the wide smile cross his face, realised just how revealing those words were. She swallowed a sudden painful lump in her throat, feeling it settle in a solid mass in her stomach.

'You noticed,' he affirmed softly. 'From the song you sang I thought you might have.' He leaned closer, his thighs in this relaxed position brushing suffocatingly against hers. 'I've had some interesting lines thrown at me over the years, but I have to admit yours are new to me.' The warmth of his green eyes surveyed the flush that spread up from the neck of her skimpy blue top to the delicate skin of her cheeks.

He seemed fascinated by it, and so was she as his hand reached out and traced across her heated skin. Her breath caught in her throat, and her pulse throbbed madly under his fingers. The eyes she raised to his were turbulent.

'Mr Lyneham . . .' She started to contradict his view of her choice of song.

'Ross, please,' he interrupted.

Momentarily distracted, Zoe blinked. 'Ross?'

He nodded assent. 'I think we can dispense with formality, don't you? After all, you approached me on the beach.'

She had thought herself unobserved, but now he was saying he had witnessed her hesitant approach, seen the way her eyes had positively devoured him. Her nerves leapt when one of his hands came to rest on hers again. The wave of heat that swept through her like a tornado left no nerve untouched. She wondered if he felt the tremor that echoed the warmth, and knew that he had when she met his eyes. Yet he had mistaken it for sexual attraction, a come-on, and not due to the deep love she had for him.

Oh, Ross, why? The despairing cry for understanding flew into her mind and closed around her heart in the seconds that golden eyes locked with green. Memories engulfed her. All the good times were being swamped by this awful change of attitude. Desperately, she knew she had to hang on to her memories and fight against his cynicism.

Gamely she rallied herself. 'Will you stop insinuating I'm cheap? If you had a bad experience, I'm not responsible for it. I'm me, and I won't let you keep on insulting me. If you have such a low opinion of me, then I can't see why you want me to have dinner with you.'

Ross laughed but it was dry, and his smile didn't reach his eyes. 'Can't you? Then I'll tell you why. You're beautiful. You're as attracted to me as I am to you. I'm looking forward to taking you to my bed where I know you won't disappoint me.'

Zoe was incensed. 'Am I supposed to be flattered?'

His look was scornful and impatient. 'You parade yourself for me in a virtually transparent bikini, seek me out in my office, then sing suggestive songs to me, and expect me to accept you're a shrinking violet?' he taunted.

Zoe slammed down the piano lid and stood up. 'You can find yourself another dinner-cum-sleeping partner, Mr Lyneham,' she cried in a mixture of disgust and mortification.

'Don't think I won't,' he shot back, coming to his feet and standing rigidly over her.

'Then do it!' she ordered, having had more than enough and battling a desire to burst into angry and bitter tears. She swung about to go, but Ross's hand shot out and hauled her back. Zoe flung her head up and glared at him, totally unaware that her golden eyes were awash and her lips were trembling. The icy depths of his eyes suddenly lost their anger and he gave a ragged sigh, releasing her arm from his painful grip and watching as she rubbed the spot defensively. The change in him was welcome, but just as mystifying, leaving her floundering.

'Zoe, I'm sorry. If it's any satisfaction to you, I'll admit I don't even like myself sometimes. Put it down to that bad experience you mentioned. Rightly or wrongly, you're bearing the brunt of it.' The explanation was grudgingly offered.

There it was again, that allusion to the singer. Zoe swallowed her tears. 'It doesn't mean we're all the same, Ross. That's being unjust. I won't be your punchbag.' Did he think she would accept everything he threw at her without a fight? Apparently so, for there was a reluctant appreciation of her stance in his eyes. Nothing she said dented his confidence.

'I take it you'll still be joining me for dinner?' he prompted.

Would she? She knew as well as he did that there was little doubt of it. 'Yes,' she admitted, coming very close to hating herself. Her ambivalent emotions confused her.

Ross smiled, the victorious male. 'Good. I'll call for you,' he stated, running a finger along her jaw, then turned and calmly walked away.

Only when he had gone did it register what he had charged her with—parading about in a transparent bikini. Could it have been true? Why not? It was a new one and probably wasn't meant to be used for swimming. She was mortified by the thought, but at the same time felt a betraying tingle of excitement. By fair means or foul she had to remind him of what they had shared. It was basic, but even the longest journeys started with one small step. She would make it work for her, this attraction, because it was the one thing they had shared that wasn't dead or forbidden to her.

She sat down again, but it was a while before she played anything, and even then they weren't happy tunes. But then she had almost forgotten what happiness was.

Zoe was approaching Mike Farrell's office some hours later, when he poked his head round the door and saw her.

'Just the person I was looking for. Telephone for you, Zoe,' he called, and disappeared inside again. Rather like a turtle, Zoe thought, with a grin.

Mike was a very nice man, who had made her welcome when she had first arrived on the island two months ago, and who had taken no offence when his attempt to build their relationship had been gently repulsed by her. She looked on him as a friend and he seemed happy to do the same with her.

The call was from Ross. Some urgent business had cropped up and he wouldn't be able to make dinner after all. He sounded too distracted and off-hand for Zoe even to attempt a conversation and she agreed to change their date to Friday instead. She heard his phone go down before she had replaced her own receiver and pulled a wry face. So much for finding her irresistible.

'Don't tell me, my old friend chose work over you,' Mike guessed accurately.

Rather despondent, Zoe nodded. 'It . . . surprised me.'

'You and a whole load of others,' Mike agreed solemnly. 'He always was single-minded about his business, but never to the extent that he let it interfere with his romances. That's only happened since the crash. He doesn't seem to—like—women as individuals as he did before. I don't know what happened, but it's sure screwed him up.'

'I had noticed,' she stated wryly.

Mike grinned. 'So you don't need me to warn you to tread lightly. Part of the trouble is, of course, that he's not getting fit quick enough. It annoys him that he can't remember those weeks before the accident and that he's still getting bad headaches. Put the two together and that means he tries too hard and gets tired too quickly. What he really needs to do is relax.' He paused and shot her a look. 'I can't field all his telephone calls, so if he should happen to get interested in something to take his mind off work, a lot of people will be forever grateful.'

Zoe smiled at his hopeful expression. 'Something being me, you mean?'

He spread his hands. 'If the situation fits.'

'I might not have much influence,' she added, recalling vividly Ross's aversion to her profession.

Mike rubbed his nose and gave a devilish grin. 'Let's just say, you have powers of persuasion unavailable to me. And if you can get him to slow down before this Doctor Vernon arrives, so much the better.'

Dr Vernon! Zoe gave an audible gasp. She didn't believe her luck could be that bad. It would be too much of a coincidence for the doctor to be other than the one she knew, and he was the very last person she wanted to know what she was doing here. On an island the size of Mariposa, what chance was there of staying out of his way?

Fortunately Mike took her agitation as a sign of worry over Ross's health and was at pains to tell her this was only a regular check-up. Zoe was grateful to take herself off to her chalet where she spent more hours than was comfortable wondering about the expected visit, and considering its implications. It was a relief when it was time to go on stage for the evening.

It was only when she was heading back to her chalet in the dark hours before dawn that she allowed her thoughts to dwell on Ross again. He was quite right about their mutual attraction. She had come seeking him because she loved him, never consciously thinking of their sexual response to each other. If Ross had been unable to make love to her with the abandon they had once enjoyed, it wouldn't have mattered. She might miss it, but he was the important thing. Without him the joy would be gone. Yet, having found him, it was the potency of their attraction which was hitting her most. It pulled at her all the time, awakening her to the knowledge of just how much she wanted to make love with him again.

It was impossible not to recall the nights they had lain in each other's arms, sated with passion. She could almost feel his hands exploring her body, and her fingers tingled as if she had his firm flesh beneath them.

But it was a wanting she would never satisfy while he had the opinions he did. Mike had said he had only acted this way after the crash, and Ross had not troubled to hide the fact that it was singers he had a down on. If she was paranoid she might even begin to believe she had something to do with it, but that was silly. Ross didn't remember her, so that ruled her out. Which only left the suggestion that some time in the last eight months he had met someone else who had dealt him a savage blow.

Zoe hated the thought that he could have met and fallen in love with another woman, but forced herself to face that possibility, and the stark realisation that one woman's actions could mean that Ross would never again trust any woman enough to fall in love with her.

Her brooding thoughts were broken into by a flicker of light through the trees beyond the staff quarters. So far as she knew, there was nothing beyond but virgin island. She turned her steps that way in idle curiosity. She was too wound up to sleep anyway.

It came as quite a surprise to walk out of the trees into a large clearing. She could just make out the shape of a long low bungalow with immaculate lawns strung out before it. The light came from one side, a room that led off from the wide veranda. The shutters were thrown wide and one was swaying in the breeze. There was no movement anywhere. Its *Mary Celeste* air made Zoe consider it needed investigation, and moved up the line of trees.

'What's wrong, Zoe?' The words coming out of the darkness behind her frightened her so much she literally jumped, spinning round in an uncontrolled turn that staggered her. She would have fallen if a convenient tree hadn't broken her fall, almost breaking her arm in the process.

It was Ross.

She was so angry at the scare he had given her that she forgot he didn't know who she was and rounded on him furiously. 'Oh God, you idiot! You nearly scared the living daylights out of me! What are you doing, running around terrorising people at this time of night?'

'And I suppose you weren't flitting around like a ghost?' he returned smartly.

'That's a stupid thing to say, Ross, and you know it! I thought there might be intruders. I was worried, but I can see you aren't,' Zoe snapped, rubbing her arm. 'I'll have a bruise the size of an ostrich egg tomorrow.'

'I suppose that's my fault too?' He sounded suspiciously as if he was having trouble quelling a laugh.

'You're darn right it was!'

There was definitely laughter as he walked a few steps nearer. 'In that case I most humbly apologise. You must let me kiss it better.' Before she could stop him, his hands had closed on her shoulders and his fair head bent to press his lips to the sore spot.

Zoe couldn't still her gasp of mingled shock and delight. His lips were firm and warm, burning the tender flesh, and she tilted her head to watch his tanned jawline move as his lips caressed her. His thick hair moved as her breath caught it and of its own volition her hand lifted to thread her fingers through the springy waves. The scent of him enveloped her, as intoxicating as wine. Her eyes closed and she drifted away, remembering the last time he had held her, of her heavy eyes watching as his head moved against her breast. Oh, darling . . .

Then Ross eased slowly away from her. 'Is that better?' he asked in a husky undertone, but his eyes, when she focused on them, were darkly mocking.

'No!' she moaned huskily, rejecting that look, her dream destroyed.

But to Ross, her words were the answer he had expected. His musing touch skated up and down her arms, sending shivers along her spine. 'Your skin is as soft as silk. I want to find out if it's the same all over this delectable body of yours.'

Zoe's heart galloped on madly, leaving her feeling as if he had done what he only spoke of doing. Every nerve was strained to a pitch of awareness of the warmth that came from his body, of the spicy scent of his cologne and the musky fragrance that was his alone. He was waiting for her to move into his arms, to signal her willingness for his voyage of discovery. It was going to be a hard battle to fight her own responses, but it had to be fought.

Emotionally and physically she took a step away from him. 'Sorry, confidential information.'

He let her go with tormenting ease. 'Oh, I'd keep it

confidential, honey. Strictly for my eyes only,' he teased outrageously. 'Did you miss me tonight?'

'About as much as you did me,' she advised him sharply.

He reached out and drew a finger over her lips. 'I think I can disprove that . . .' He pulled her against him before she realised what he was about, and his lips descended on hers.

Gently they rubbed and lifted, dropping again to take her lower lip between his teeth and tug at its fulness, parting it from its mate. With a tremor she felt his tongue lightly caress the soft inner skin and then the precious touch was removed.

'Satisfied?' Ross questioned, his voice pitched low.

Zoe swallowed painfully. He knew she wasn't. As soon as he had felt the betraying cling of her lips he had drawn away, leaving her burning inside.

'You proved your point,' she confirmed huskily.

'So, having proved I missed you, will you give me a straight answer?' he prompted.

'Yes, I missed you,' Zoe admitted on a soft sigh. She looked up at him in concern, recalling why he had cancelled. 'Ross, you surely didn't work all night?'

'Not all night. I had a headache and couldn't sleep. I was intending to go to bed when I saw you creeping about like Modesty Blaise. For your information, I live in the bungalow.'

He laughed, and the sound sent warm shivers through her. Her senses, already heightened by his shock arrival and the intimate brush of his lips, had no defence against the overwhelming attraction that was Ross Lyneham. Especially when he pulled her into the circle of his arms once more, his hands at the small of her back pressing her gently into the firm warmth of his body.

'If you're . . . not well,' she haltingly tried to

concentrate on what he had said and not on how her thighs moulded themselves to his, making her vitally aware of his maleness, 'perhaps you ought to go straight to bed.'

'You are so right. And there's one sure-fire way of making certain I do as you tell me—you can come with me.' His words completed the rout, and she melted, her good intentions forgotten.

Ross tightened his hold, and with her lower body locked firmly against his, Zoe could not hold back the tide of longing that burned like a bushfire from her stomach to every tingling nerve. She felt the stirring of his body through the thin silk of her dress and instinct urged her into the betraying movement of her hips. A sighing moan tore itself from low in her throat and her hands splayed out against the firm muscles of his chest, feeling the heat and throb of life through his shirt.

'Is that yes?' his voice murmured huskily into her ear as his lips toyed with her lobe, pulling the tender skin and drawing it into his mouth.

Zoe groaned inwardly. Why did his attraction have to be so damned potent? 'You make it hard for a girl to say no.'

'It's only hard when you really want to say yes,' Ross replied, his hands travelling slowly down to her thighs then up again. All the while his lips plundered the soft skin of her nape.

She wanted so much to say yes that it felt as if something vital was being torn out of her. It was too soon. He felt nothing for her but desire, whereas she . . . 'No, Ross,' her tormented voice denied them both. 'Whatever impression I may have given you on the beach, I'm just not like that.'

His nuzzling ceased, and Zoe wasn't sure whether to be sorry or grateful. 'What impression would that be?'

His apparently sincere question was ruined by barely concealed merriment.

'As if you didn't know! That damn bikini!' she burst out in an agony of angry embarrassment.

His maddening laughter was salt in the wound. She was instantly furious, and, determined not to remain in his arms a moment longer, Zoe struggled to be released so that she could leave in a fine show of indignation. But Ross merely hauled her in to the solid wall of his chest again and anchored her there until she wore herself out with her struggles. When at last she was still he astounded her by apologising.

'I'm sorry. You really are embarrassed, aren't you? You're more vulnerable than you look.' He studied her curiously, as if she were some unknown species.

Zoe ground her teeth, wishing she had never mentioned it, even if it had successfully cooled the atmosphere. 'Not at all. I just didn't know it would . . . do that.'

Ross was still having difficulty keeping a straight face, 'It was an . . . inspiring . . . sight.'

Zoe put on a brave face. 'Well, if nothing else, it's taught me to look at labels,' she declared, attempting to leave his weakened hold. 'Now I'm going to bed.'

'If that's another invitation, my dear Zoe, I'd very much like to join you.' His silky-smooth voice ran molten havoc through her defences.

Oh, don't do this to me, Ross, she begged silently. It was all she could do to remain looking up at him as if he hadn't turned her whole system upside-down again.

Ross stared into her upturned face with peculiar intensity, for once neither mocking nor teasing. She was wondering if he had found what he was looking for, when he sighed. 'You look tired. I'd better let you get some sleep. But Zoe, I'll take a raincheck on that offer.' Ross pushed her gently away in the direction of the trees.

Zoe took two uncertain steps then stopped to glance back at him. He stood watching her with his arms crossed over his chest. His behaviour had been more like the Ross she remembered, which made his changes of mood even more incomprehensible.

Even in the darkness he seemed to pick up her inner turmoil, and his voice when he spoke was almost gentle. 'What is it?'

Zoe swallowed, tears threatening again. 'Oh, nothing,' she murmured, unconsciously wistful, 'just ... goodnight.'

She left him then, suddenly feeling the chill of her fears in the cool night air. She felt very tired, drained of that restless energy which had kept her going these last terrible months. But her bed, that had been her sanctuary, now helped to plague her exhausted brain with memories. She tossed restlessly as the good dreams turned to the horror of that fateful day when all her hopes had been torn along with the twisted metal.

Would the nightmare never end?

CHAPTER THREE

ZOE awoke much later than usual next day. Knowing she needed some violent exercise to banish her bad dreams, she took herself off for a swim. She had hoped it might also keep her thoughts off Ross and her worries about how to get through to him, but he was the first person she saw on the virtually empty stretch of beach as she waded ashore some fifteen minutes later. He had just emerged from the sea himself, and water still dripped from his magnificent tanned body.

Her eyes wandered up his long legs, past the disgracefully small briefs and on to his heaving chest. She stood rooted to the spot drinking him in, and he looked so beautiful to her that a broad smile swept across her face. God, she had been so lonely all these months, she could hardly believe she was here with him now.

She walked slowly to where she had left her towel and found another spread beside it. It had to belong to Ross. He must have followed her down here. It was a thought to make her heart beat faster. She dropped down and sat watching him walk towards her, hugging her knees with her arms. When his tall frame came to a halt before her, blocking out the sun, she tipped her head up.

'Hi.' He smiled down at her, wiping water from his eyes.

He seemed disposed to be friendly but she knew from experience that might not last. Her smile back was guarded. It was difficult to behave completely naturally with him. 'Hello. How do you feel today?'

Ross flung himself down on his towel, stretching his

long legs and resting on an elbow to watch her. 'I've had better mornings, but the swim helped.'

Close to, he was temptation, so ruggedly male and relaxed. She let her eyes wander back to the moving surface of the sea. 'I love the water. I used to spend hours in the sea when I was little.'

'Me too. Were you an only child?'

Zoe rested her chin on her knees. It felt odd to be telling him things he knew but had forgotten. 'No, I have an older brother who's in the RAF, and a younger sister at university. And you?' It was equally odd to ask him questions and pretend she didn't know the answers.

'I have a younger brother, Jack. He's a lawyer.'

'For the company?'

'No, he deals with criminal cases. If you ever need a good lawyer, I can recommend him.'

She turned her head at that to quiz him, 'Do you think I'm likely to?'

His teeth flashed whitely against his tan as he grinned. 'Always be prepared, that's my motto.'

'You were never a boy scout!' Zoe choked in disbelief. A picture flashed before her eyes of Ross in short shorts and funny hat, and she collapsed back on her towel, creased up with mirth.

Ross loomed over her. 'What's so amusing?' he demanded, and when she told him between giggles, his face was a study. 'So, you think it's safe to laugh at me, do you? There's a mighty long drop beneath that tightrope you're walking. I might just take it into my head to knock you off it.'

With a last chuckle she subsided on a shaky sigh, amazed by the change in him from the last couple of days. He was so much more relaxed and approachable. She caught his eye and the glowing embers behind his green gaze started flash-fires on her skin. 'Promises,

promises,' she gibed softly.

For a moment she couldn't explain the look that passed across his face, and then he grinned. 'How you do love to tease. Last night stop, this morning go. Aren't you afraid you might push my restraint to the limit?'

'What can you do to me here?' She looked to where a group of bathers had appeared.

His smile was devilish and the leaping lights were back in his eyes. 'You'd be surprised. I could take you into the water and make love to you and nobody would ever guess.'

Her breathing was suddenly very shallow and her limbs became heavy and languorous. From somewhere she dredged a provocative retort. 'Well, if I ever run out of ideas, I'll certainly keep that in mind.'

A reluctant laugh echoed her glib words. 'You aren't going to flatter my ego at all, are you?'

'No, you don't need it.' With movements that were strangely jerky, Zoe sat up again. 'If I started to flatter you, you'd accuse me of having an ulterior motive.'

Ross sat up beside her. 'Such as having designs on my wealthy bachelor status. Well honey, I wasn't born yesterday, and there's no trick you can try that I haven't come across. Remember that and this little affair could be to your advantage.' Instantly the friendly atmosphere was destroyed.

Zoe turned her head away, blinking rapidly. 'I am not after your money.'

'That makes you pretty unique.' Ross stated, patently disbelieving.

Unused to having her motives doubted, Zoe twisted back to face him. 'That's what I keep telling you.'

Ross studied her serious face, with its overbright eyes of molten gold. He captured her hand and sank back, taking her with him so that she ended up lying across his chest. A curling warmth invaded her as she came into intimate contact with his powerfully muscled torso. His body heat scorched her, awakening a taut need that craved the silken glide of his hands to satisfy it. His fingers slipped into her hair, framing her head. 'Mm, just keep telling me. You never know, it might even restore my faith in women.'

It was a challenge any woman would want to take up—to make a doubting man trust—but Zoe saw the hardness in his eyes.

'Oh, Ross, what did she do?' It was a despairing cry, not really expecting an answer.

Immediately Ross tensed in anger. He reversed their positions so that she was crushed beneath his weight. 'Forget her—I have,' he ordered bleakly, then his lips closed over hers and, for stormy minutes, all thought of everything was swept from her mind. His mouth plundered hers, not asking for a response as his tongue probed in erotically explicit parody. It wasn't a kiss of respect and Zoe despised herself for her inability to remain unmoved.

When he raised his head, Ross studied her flushed cheeks and swollen lips with satisfaction. 'This is all we need. Nothing else matters. Your past and mine aren't important. I want you and you want me, that's all there is, and it's real.'

Zoe's hands bunched into fists on his shoulders. 'What about love?'

His lips twisted scornfully. 'An overworked euphemism for want. You're going to tell me you believe in it?'

'Yes, I do,' she asserted hardily.

He laughed, lifting himself up and away from her. 'It's about as real as the Tooth Fairy and Santa Claus. But then your sort are used to hiding behind fairy tales.'

Zoe didn't have to ask, she understood his insult very

well. 'It's just as well there's no likelihood of my falling in love with you then, isn't it?' Even voicing the lie was a betrayal. She watched as Ross climbed to his feet, shaking out his towel and draping it around his neck.

'Good,' he stated shortly. 'I want you, Zoe, but that's as far as it goes.' And, having warned her off, Ross turned and strode away, his long legs soon carrying him from view.

Zoe didn't turn and watch him go. Tears were already streaming down her face. It wasn't till much later that she straightened from her forlorn position and went back to her own chalet.

She didn't see Ross again until that evening. She had barely started her performance when the sensitive hairs on her neck began to tingle, sending a ripple of awareness down her spine, and she knew he was there. It took an effort not to swivel round to discover just where he was, but she resisted the impulse.

It was easier a little later, between songs, to sweep the audience while they were applauding a medley. He was closer to the stage this time, but still discreetly apart from the rest of the room, and he was not alone. He was deep in conversation with an exquisite redhead. Even as Zoe watched, the woman put her hand on his arm in a little intimate gesture, and their heads dipped so close she could almost swear a kiss had been exchanged.

Pain, sharp and destructive, tore through her on a wave of jealousy. She wanted to scream that he had no right to be with another woman, and was appalled at her own violence. She forced herself to look away before anyone could witness the pallor of her cheeks and her pinched lips.

She tried not to think of the pair of them sitting just yards away, but it was impossible. While she sang her mind visualised them, and in between her eyes constantly strayed to their table and her anger and pain grew worse. Oh, God! Why had she assumed she was the only one? The island was full of beautiful women, so why should he limit himself? Because he was hers. The words scorched themselves into her brain. Just as she was his. He had no right to do this. Yet she recognised the futility of thinking that way when he had no idea of who she was. Even so, it hurt. She had never been jealous of the women in Ross's past because they had been exactly that, but this was something else, something she couldn't ignore.

Once she glanced across only to find they were both watching her, smiling and applauding along with the rest, and Ross inclined his head, lifting his glass in a silent toast. Zoe gritted her teeth and plastered on her most professional smile, and for her own peace of mind resolutely refused to look in Ross's direction at all.

When she stopped for a break, her nerves were at fever-pitch. Off stage she found the head waiter coming to meet her. When he delivered Ross's request for her to join him, she was momentarily rocked back on her heels, and her first defensive reaction was to refuse. Then pride came to her rescue. How could she ignore what wasn't really a request without looking extremely foolish? Ross in his present mood would find something mocking to say and she wanted to avoid calling sarcasm down on her head. All she could do was grin and bear it.

As she approached the table, Ross rose to his feet to hold out a chair for her. He raised a quizzical eyebrow when she thanked him coolly and sat down. Her failure to respond to his smile drew a sardonic twist to his lips as he reseated himself.

The redhead was even more stunning close to, her eyes the largest and bluest Zoe had ever seen. And she was poured into a designer dress that clung in all the right places. Her jewellery was unobtrusive but platinum without a doubt. One look told Zoe she couldn't compete with this.

To make it worse, she greeted Zoe with a friendly, open smile. 'Thank you for agreeing to join us. I so enjoyed your singing, I absolutely had to insist Ross invite you over.' Her voice turned out to be as vibrant as her hair.

'Louise is a self-confessed blues fan,' Ross added, deftly filling three glasses from the bottle in the cooler beside him.

Louise nodded, accepting a glass. 'Yes, indeed. I was telling Ross that I'd heard you sing in London, wasn't I, darling?' She turned to Ross for confirmation, her pink-tipped fingers resting on his suited arm.

Zoe watched the manoeuvre staking claim to him and intercepted the benevolent smile he cast at his companion. Jealousy left a bitter taste in her mouth. She accepted her glass of wine, swallowing a mouthful without tasting it.

'You're quite famous in your own way.' Ross slanted her a considering look from narrow watchful eyes.

'Which is better than being infamous,' Zoe retorted sharply, too hurt to guard her tongue.

Ross's eyes widened with amusement. 'Is that aimed at anyone we know?'

Zoe smiled grimly. 'Make a wild guess.'

Ross laughed, in no doubt who she was referring to, but Louise took it as gospel and recited a list of famous names that she thought might fit. Zoe's eyebrows shot up and she blinked at Ross in surprise. He returned her look blandly.

'Beautiful, isn't she?'

Zoe looked at Louise, who had stopped speaking, and saw a fleeting glimpse of light which passed too quickly for her to grasp. 'Quite exquisite.' And totally ingenuous by the looks of it.

Louise lacked vanity too. 'Oh, I'm really quite ordinary, and I have no talent. Whereas Zoe is truly amazing.'

Ross captured her hand and raised it to his lips. 'Which statement makes mine all the more true, darling,' he declared warmly.

Zoe couldn't disagree with him. It didn't take more than five minutes to realise Louise was a genuinely nice woman. She took another hasty sip of her drink and caught Ross watching her, a curious expression of—waiting—in his eyes. Waiting for what, and why?

'Darling, you've been saying the sweetest things to me ever since you picked me up this afternoon,' Louise laughed softly.

Zoe's breath left her in a whoosh, just as if someone had hit her in the stomach. Now she understood, and her jealousy disappeared beneath a wave of anger and hurt. She swallowed hard and forced herself to sound natural.

'Ross picked you up?'

Louise chuckled. 'Literally.'

'And figuratively. I wasn't going to miss the opportunity of having your company,' Ross teased gallantly.

'I couldn't get the hang of my sailboard.' Louise ignored his interruption. 'I was more often in the sea than on it, but Ross kept picking me up and putting me back until I got it right. He was determined I should do it.'

'Yes, Ross is nothing if not determined,' Zoe gritted out hardily, shooting him a look of dislike which rebounded harmlessly off his bland expression. She returned her attention to the other woman. 'Will you be here long, Louise?'

'I go home tomorrow, unfortunately.'

Zoe looked sympathetic. 'What a pity.' Her scathing look she saved for Ross. 'You'll be losing your friend so soon.'

'There are plenty more fish in the sea,' Ross shrugged.

'At least Louise will have escaped the sharks,' Zoe went on acidly.

'Goodness, are there sharks?' Louise gasped, going white.

Zoe laughed grimly. 'Oh yes, and even some of the finned variety.'

Louise looked from one to the other of them. 'I don't understand.'

Ross shot Zoe a look cold enough to freeze an iceberg before turning a warm smile on the other woman. 'Sometimes Zoe talks in riddles.'

'I'd be only *too* happy to explain,' Zoe goaded sweetly.

Ross's hand came down hard on hers as it rested on the table top. 'All right, you spitting little cat. You can sheathe your claws right now or you won't like what will happen next,' he bit off harshly.

Zoe flushed a deep red and heard a gasp from Louise. 'I don't like what's gone before,' she snapped back, engaging in a silent tussle to retrieve her hand.

'I already guessed that.' Ross quelled her without apparent effort, and Zoe was forced to give up or indulge in an unpleasant scene.

'Have I missed something?' Louise asked doubtfully.

Zoe looked at her and decided that such an ingenuous woman needed to be put right on one or two points. 'Yes, you did. Perhaps I should tell you . . .'

Ross stood up abruptly, dragging Zoe with him. 'Would you excuse us a moment, Louise. I have something to say to Zoe that just won't wait.' He spoke with angry politeness and barely waited for Louise's bemused agreement before steering Zoe backstage.

'Why the hell did you do that?' he demanded furiously, pushing Zoe back against the wall and trapping her there with his arms. 'Louise would have been hurt.'

What about me? Zoe cried silently. I'm hurting all the time.

'You shouldn't have started it,' she challenged, fuelling her anger to hide her bruises.

Ross stood back, stuffing his hands carelessly into his trouser pockets, arching one elegant brow in interrogation. 'Started what?'

Zoe clenched her hands into fists. 'You were using her to show me just how little claim I had on you. Well, you needn't have bothered. I already got the message, loud and clear.'

'From our conversation earlier I decided you needed it underlined,' Ross admitted his strategy with a hard stare.

She had guessed as much. She had talked of love and he had decided to warn her off, callously using the innocent Louise. But why had he done it? What was he afraid of? Was the warning for her or himself? Was she already getting too close, bringing into question his own convictions? She just didn't know.

'You shouldn't have used her,' she stated flatly.

'No,' Ross acceded, 'she's too nice for that. As it is, there's no harm done.'

Oh God! I'm bleeding to death and you can't even see the knife you cut me with! Zoe felt hysterical laughter bubbling up inside her and knew she had to get away quickly.

'So, what happens now?' she asked tonelessly.

'We go on as before,' Ross stated, watching her closely, frowning when she returned his look with a strangely bleak, lost one of her own. 'Nothing's changed.

I still want you, and you wouldn't have been so angry if you didn't still want me. Only now we know exactly where we stand.'

'Of course! How silly of me.'

One large hand came out and framed her jaw. 'Convince me it's what you want and I'll leave you entirely alone.'

Her silence was his answer, even though his cynical amusement twisted the knife even deeper. The only thing she had to hold on to was the flare of attraction between them. If she ever met the woman who had turned him from a warm-hearted man to this hardened stranger, she would kill her with her bare hands.

'You'd better get back to Louise,' Zoe suggested woodenly. 'Even she could come up with the right answer, given time to think.'

Ross's smile was enigmatic. 'I'll be in touch.'

Zoe watched him walk away, wishing heartily she didn't have to go back on stage and act as if nothing had happened, but she had no choice. She was a professional and the show had to go on. Only she knew her heart wasn't in it. She had left that with a golden-haired, green-eyed man who had stated all too clearly that he didn't now, and never would, want it.

Two days later, Zoe was convinced she was being punished for her actions. It seemed ridiculous, and maybe she was wrong, but she didn't think so. Ross had been conspicuous by his absence, and she could think of only one reason for that. She had to know her place in the scheme of things and not make waves.

Standing at her small sink, up to her elbows in soapsuds and washing, Zoe chewed on her lip. She knew how she had felt when she couldn't see Ross, but he showed no similar compulsion to seek her out. If he didn't see her it wouldn't be the end of his world, was the statement he was making. Only it hadn't always been like that. She let her thoughts drift miles away, back to Crete when a different Ross showed her in countless different ways that he loved her. She could feel his arms sliding around her, drawing her into him as they stood watching the tide, feel the warm brush of his lips against her nape and her ears and his sensually smooth voice teasing her senses.

'Mm . . . nice.'

Her lips curved as the feeling of security his arms represented enfolded her again. She welcomed the probe of fingers against the fluttering skin of her stomach, but it was when they began gliding upwards to the velvet underside of her breast that her gaze lowered and encountered tanned flesh.

Shock sent her rigid, reality staining her cheeks bright red—for what had begun as a daydream had turned into fact and she looked down in horror at the arms that held her. Embarrassment gave her strength and she positively lept away from her captor.

'Ross!'

'The very same.' He had let her go and now he turned her round, ignoring the soap suds that dripped from her hands on to his feet. 'You seemed pleased to see me,' he teased.

'I was miles away,' she gasped, absurdly pleased to see him, but determined he shouldn't know it for treating her so carelessly.

'I know, but delightfully warm and responsive,' he grinned back, raffishly.

'That's why you stayed away, isn't it?' she probed, speaking before she had time to think better of it.

Ross shook his head and tutted. 'Naughty, your claws are showing again, darling. Enchanting as you undeniably are, dear Zoe, I came to Mariposa on business, not to gad about.'

'In that case, are you sure you can spare me the time?' she demanded, reaching for a towel and drying her hands. She watched a little breathlessly as Ross's charming smile spread across his face.

'Oh, I always make time for a beautiful woman, tiger-eyes,' he drawled seductively. 'Come and join me for a walk,' he urged.

'Are you sure it's me you want?' she asked doubtfully. After all, their last meeting hadn't been exactly friendly.

A devilish grin twitched his lips. 'I most definitely want you,' he assured her with quite another meaning.

Zoe took a deep breath as her insides melted. 'I meant, after the other evening.'

For a moment a grimness entered his eyes then was gone. 'We both said a lot of things, which cleared the air. Now let's forget it. Are you going to come with me?'

She didn't altogether agree with his assessment, but after only the briefest pause she nodded. Ross was wearing white shorts and shirt, so her own lemon shorts and tee-shirt were quite adequate. She slipped on her sandals, ran a comb through her hair and was ready in under a minute. His smile was appreciative of her lack of primping.

They set off through the grounds in the general direction of the tennis courts. It was pleasant simply walking with him, but after a while Zoe felt compelled to break the silence.

'Why are you being so pleasant today?' she queried, crossing her fingers in the hope it would stop him taking offence.

It seemed to work. 'Aren't I usually?' he teased, slipping an arm about her waist, the warmth of his hand resting possessively on her hip.

Zoe cast him an old-fashioned look, trying to ignore the fact that his touch made her pulses leap.

Ross laughed down at her. 'If I'm so awful, why did you come with me?'

There was no real answer to that. 'Well, I never said I was intelligent,' she laughed back.

They passed the courts and headed down a path into the trees.

'Actually it occurred to me that perhaps I was being unfair to you,' Ross eventually answered her question.

'Only perhaps?' she interrogated, and in looking up at him she tripped over an exposed root and fell headlong, taking a surprised Ross with her.

It was fortunate for her that he did, for by some gymnastic feat he managed to land beneath her and cushion her fall. Winded, they stared at each other, then Ross began to laugh, a full-bodied rumble of pleasure.

'You didn't have to be so subtle, darling. If you wanted to be in my arms you should have asked me,' he taunted cheerfully.

'Ooh!' Zoe fumed, deeply embarrassed. She tried to get up but Ross neatly swung her over so that he was kneeling astride her hips, one hand planted either side of her head.

'Going somewhere?' he mocked. Her ineffective bucking, far from making him release her, had the effect of bringing their bodies into close contact. Heart-stoppingly so.

Tension began to build between them as they watched each other closely. Zoe could feel her own heart thudding faster by the second, and she could quite clearly see the rapid pulse-beat at the base of Ross's strong neck.

She licked her lips, striving to hold on to her control. 'Let me up.'

Amusement twisted the corners of his attractive mouth. 'I'm quite comfortable.'

'I just knew you were shifty,' she accused, taking deep breaths to steady herself because Ross had just moulded his hands to her shoulders and was leaning down even closer. Her voice turned to a squeak. 'You aren't playing fair!'

Coming to a halt a breath away, Ross studied the flush on her cheeks. 'Who's playing? This is a very serious position you're in, sweetheart.'

'It's not fair!' she wailed, unbearably tempted by the male lips so close to hers. When he smiled this close, Zoe could see how his eyes crinkled at the corners. It kept her mesmerised.

'Give me a good reason why I should let you go.'

Heart beating like a drum, and with her breasts rising and falling with her rapid breathing, Zoe's brain took a holiday. If truth be told, she didn't want him to let her go—now or ever. She didn't know why he was so different today, he must have some ulterior motive of his own, but whatever it was she couldn't quarrel with it. She wanted him to kiss her quite desperately. Longed to feel the length of him against her once more.

Her arms were actually stealing around his neck when the 'Oh, excuse us,' followed by an embarrassed cough, brought their heads round. An elderly couple had been halted by their two bodies across the track. With a charming apology, Ross came to his feet and helped Zoe to hers, smoothing over the moment with aplomb. Zoe watched the couple's silent progress until they disappeared, feeling totally disconcerted. She thanked goodness they hadn't happened along any later, for who knew what they might have witnessed?

She glanced at Ross, only to find him leaning negligently against a tree, arms folded over his chest, struggling with a laugh and looking incredibly sexy. Ross pushed himself away from his support. Crossing the short space that separated them, he took her hips between his hands before she could move back and pulled her close against the firm thrust of his thighs.

'Now, where were we?' His voice was little more than a husky whisper breathed against her forehead.

Held as close to him as she was, Zoe could not fail to be aware of his desire for her. She attempted to wriggle from his grip, unsuccessfully. 'May I remind you this is still a public place?' she said in a breathless little rush before his closeness made her lose the use of her voice completely.

Ross stilled her efforts without much trouble. His voice was rich with amusement when he next spoke close to her ear. 'You talk too much.'

Zoe looked up at him, aware of the subtle excitement that made her skin receptive to even the slightest brush of his, and set her heart clamouring in her chest. It was too strong to fight. 'Then you'd better shut me up,' she declared, surrendering.

'That's the best offer I've had all day.' Ross smiled down at her, then slowly, slowly, he lowered his mouth to hers.

His lips were warm and seductive, drowning her in memories his other kisses had come nowhere near evoking. Teasing and tempting, his searching kisses drew a response she wanted to give. She melted into his arms, her hands locking in the thick wave of hair at his nape, as she returned his kiss with fervour. She welcomed the firm imprint of his strong frame along the whole length of her body, and a shivering response trembled through her.

It seemed impossible to be closer to him, but Ross groaned low in his throat and his strong arms welded her to him. Zoe was conscious only of his touch, his lips burning hers and his hands spreading across her back. Her heart was pounding crazily in her chest and echoed the tattoo Ross's beat out. She felt hot and feverish, a prickly heat spreading to every sensitive pore. She surrendered to the need to rediscover the man she had loved so much and for so long.

Ross trembled too beneath her searching hands. He couldn't disguise his desire and Zoe wanted to feel it—to know she evoked the same abandoned response in him as he did in her. Her control was non-existent, need overriding every other emotion, and she sensed Ross was fast losing his too.

She wasn't surprised when he pulled away from her, holding her safely at arm's length. His eyes had darkened and burnt hotly as he studied the result of his assault on her flushed face.

'Do you always respond like that?' His voice was still husky with remembered passion.

Her eyes searched his for any sign of mockery but found nothing save a scarcely banked-down desire. 'No,' she answered him honestly.

Ross smiled but it was strangely strained. 'If you'd said anything else I wouldn't have been responsible,' he threatened darkly. 'Now I suggest a postponement until we're alone. I don't propose making love to you where anyone can come along and trip over us. I prefer comfort to vicarious thrills.'

Zoe had to smile, 'That's a relief.'

'What, no argument? I expected at least a verbal barrage for suggesting taking you to bed,' Ross provoked, tracing the line of her cheek with a finger.

'So long as you believe I don't jump into bed at the drop of a hat.' Zoe held his gaze steadily.

Ross raked a hand through his hair and eased the

tension from his shoulders. 'How many lovers you've had isn't important. I don't expect celibacy when I don't practise it myself,' he replied, his face closed.

He had hardly answered her question but Zoe couldn't press the point. If she did, she knew she would dislike the answer more than the one he had given. She had been foolish to expect anything else, considering the opinion he held of her profession. It would be up to her to prove him wrong.

She managed to keep her smile in place. 'That's generous of you,' she said in a voice not totally devoid of acid.

His frown said he hadn't missed it. 'Would you prefer I adopt a double standard?'

'No.' Of course she didn't, what woman would? It was just that he still managed to imply she was far more worldly than she really was. Unfortunately it was something very hard to prove. Her response to him wasn't innocent, and worked against her because he wasn't disposed to believe her.

Feeling decidedly uncomfortable, she said, 'Shall we go on?'

Ross slipped his arm across her shoulders. 'I have a better idea. Being alone with you is too much of a temptation right now. Why don't we play a game of tennis instead. At least that way we'll get rid of this pent-up energy,' he suggested wryly.

Zoe thought it a good idea. She would have agreed to anything rather than have to contend with her depressing thoughts about his attitude. 'I'd like that.'

Ross grinned. 'Are you always this accommodating?'

She shook her head. 'No, so you'd better take advantage of it while it lasts.' Her choice of words, she realised, could have been better.

Rather to her surprise, Ross chose not to pick her up

on them. 'In that case, you can make the coffee later,' was all he said.

Whatever his reasons, Ross did and said nothing to spoil the remainder of the day, and for once Zoe was able to relax almost completely. He went out of his way to be amusing. She hadn't laughed so much for a long, long time. Steering clear of anything personal, he was so much like the old Ross that she had to remind herself quite firmly that it wasn't so. Nevertheless, he was making sure that nothing disturbed the even tenor of the day. At least he hadn't lost the ability to enjoy himself. For a time she had come close to thinking there was nothing in the new Ross that she recognised, but she was thankful to find she had been wrong.

To cap it all, there was a single ruby-red hibiscus blossom waiting for her in her chalet when she finished her act that night. There was no note with it, but Zoe knew there was only one person it would have come from.

She wasn't stupid enough to believe in a sudden change of heart, but perhaps it did signal a willingness for a new beginning. She was smiling when she fell asleep.

CHAPTER FOUR

IT was because she was feeling happier that Zoe forgot
the imminent arrival of Dr John Vernon on the island
and, as luck would have it, he was the very person she
bumped into as she left the restaurant after breakfast
next day. They collided and cannoned off each other as if
they had practised the manoeuvre down to a fine art.
Although Zoe was by no means small, he was larger, and
if he hadn't darted out a hand to catch her, she would
have landed in an ignominious heap at his feet. This sort
of thing, she decided ruefully, was getting to be a habit.

The good doctor, in ignorance of whom he had so
nearly bowled over, began to apologise. 'I'm so sorry, I
do beg your pardon.' His well modulated voice tailed off
as he saw her face when she straightened up. His tone
and facial expression were every bit as intimidating as
she had expected. 'Good heavens, it's you, Zoe! What
the devil are you doing here? No, on second thoughts,
there's no need to answer that. This is the most crassly
irresponsible thing to do. Have you any idea of the
trouble you can cause?'

John Vernon's tall, imposing figure was stiff with
outrage. He had been caring for Zoe from the moment of
her first and only visit to the hospital, and had been quite
firm in his advice that she must under no circumstances
contact Ross until he gave his approval. A dedicated
man, he took Zoe's flouting of his words as a personal
affront. Watching the colour rise in his cheeks, Zoe
knew he was only getting started, for she had been
through it all before. The last thing she needed was to be

reminded in the middle of a busy hotel. There was nobody in sight now, but that could change in seconds. When angry, and there would be no doubting that he was, the doctor was no respecter of place or person.

'Please, John, not here,' Zoe begged, taking his arm urgently. 'You have every right to be angry with me, but not here.' The sound of a door opening and Mike's easily recognisable voice issuing from around a corner of the corridor strengthened her efforts to drag him away. 'Come with me.' Much to her surprise and relief, he did as she asked.

She led him to the small room behind the nightclub's stage that she and Marian shared. It was little more than a shoebox but at least they would be private. With the door shut on them, Zoe turned nervously to face John Vernon's uncompromising figure. She knew she needed his approval with the same amount of certainty that told her it would be far from easy to get.

'An explanation please, Zoe,' he demanded softly but firmly.

She spread her hands in a gesture of appeal. 'I had to come.'

The grim look about his mouth and eyes was daunting. 'I was under the impression that we had an agreement, Zoe.'

'And I've kept to it,' she defended sharply.

'If you had you wouldn't be here, my dear.' He went to her and placed his large hands upon her shoulders. 'Zoe, Zoe, I know it's hard . . .' he began in exasperation, but got no further before he was interrupted.

'How can you know? It isn't happening to you!' she challenged in a choked voice, looking up into his wrinkled face with its kindly grey eyes and mass of greying hair.

'I'm not without feeling or compassion, Zoe,' he

chided her for her outburst.

'Then let me do this, please.' Frantically she searched his eyes for any sign of softening.

John sighed and gave her a little shake. 'But it's wrong, my dear.'

Zoe pulled away. 'Oh God, I'm so sick of hearing that. It's always wrong, or too risky, or any one of a hundred other excuses!' Her anger and despair were too deep now for the relief of tears, and Zoe turned away to lean against the small dressing-table. After a second or two, when he made no attempt to speak, she gave a deep sigh. 'I'm sorry, John. But you have to understand. It's been eight months and I just couldn't sit and do nothing any longer. I took a calculated risk, that's all.'

'A risk that wasn't, and isn't, yours to take, young lady.' John's reply was unconditionally condemning.

As always, when this point in their arguments was reached, she bristled. 'Are you still saying I have no rights at all?'

'Until they can be substantiated, no,' he told her baldly, not attempting to pull his punch.

Zoe flinched, and bit her lip to still its trembling. 'I don't accept that. I never have and I never will,' she stated furiously. She sank down on to the stool and rested her head wearily on her arms. 'Can't you see this is killing me. What am I supposed to do? Just stop loving someone as if it were no more than a headache?'

John came and rested his tall frame against the wall beside her. 'Zoe, if I didn't know how extraordinarily patient you've already been, I'd be tempted to lose all patience with you. Can't you wait a little longer?'

'Tell me, what harm can I do now?' Zoe's voice was muffled against her hands. She had accepted all his other arguments while she waited at home in London. Had waited stoically for the right moment—which never seemed to arrive. What would he use this time, and had she the strength to fight it?

'Having talked to Ross, and now you, I take it he didn't remember you,' he said thoughtfully.

'Would I be in this position if he had?' she answered dully.

He let out an exasperated breath, but controlled his temper. 'There were no signs of stress when I examined him, and he tells me the headaches are intermittent. So in answer to your question I would say, very little after this length of time.' He gave his considered opinion. 'It's a pity, I was rather hoping for a breakthrough. The mind is a complicated piece of machinery, so you never can tell. Are you sure there was no glimmer, no hesitation?'

She raised eyes darkened by misery to his. 'John, I've been watching him like a hawk. There was nothing. Nothing.'

His hand closed comfortingly on her shoulder. 'I'm sorry you had to face it, my dear. That doesn't mean I'm any less angry at your irresponsible way of going about things. As it is, no harm has been done. But you didn't know that before you came here.'

'I admit it, and while there was still a chance that I could cause some harm I stayed away. You know that, John. But after all this time, when I knew the immediate danger was passed, I had to come. I read all I could about amnesia and I listened to every word you said. I tried to minimise the danger as much as possible. When I told you I took a calculated risk, I meant it. My risk.'

'But what if nothing changes, if . . .' he stopped mid-sentence and looked at her, at last, with comprehension. 'I see.' The two words were long drawn out. 'Zoe, I'm more sorry than I can say. You stand to lose so much.'

Her smile was watery but confident. 'Yes, but there

comes a point when you cease waiting for destiny to find you, and go out to meet it. It seemed to me I could spend the rest of my life waiting. I remember a wise old lady once saying, "Lose, but on your own terms," and that's what I'm prepared to do. My terms, not theirs.'

'His family don't know you're here?' His concern only confirmed her own fears. If John thought it wise to remain incognito, then the threat from the family was still as strong as ever.

'Nobody knows I'm here, save for Mum and Dad, and now you. I thought it safest.'

They exchanged a look full of understanding. 'Very wise,' he admitted drolly.

Zoe smiled again. 'I need all the time I can get if I'm to win Ross back to me.'

'And if you lose?'

'Then I'll know,' she murmured softly. 'Oh, I'll probably scream and shout at the injustice of it all. Then I'll go out and start the rest of my life—alone.'

'My dear girl, you don't know what will happen.' All John's earlier antagonism was gone now, and he sounded almost horrified at her prospects.

Once she had said it, and dealt with the pain of actually voicing the fear that never left her, Zoe began to feel a measure of peace. 'You can't give me any guarantees, nobody could. I have to plan, to be positive, because I won't be pitied.'

'It was a cruel accident. Nobody could imagine it happening this way. Of course, an ounce of compassion from certain parties wouldn't have gone amiss. So,' he watched her take a quick glance in the mirror to repair damages, 'you're going to say nothing?'

Zoe awarded him a smile that shone from within. 'No, but I have faith. Don't you see, it's all there, locked in. I've lost the key to one door, but there's nothing to say I can't find the key to another.'

John coughed, her fervent words and the warmth in her expression made it hard for him to dampen her hopes, as his own experience of such cases insisted he should. 'Well, I'll wish you all the luck in the world.'

He didn't add that she would need it; Zoe knew that for herself.

'Does that mean I have your blessing to stay?' She grinned at him cheekily, knowing she didn't need to ask but liking the idea of actually hearing him say so.

He snorted, recognising her tactics and disliking, as always, to be put on the spot. 'I can't stop you, I suppose. Very well, Zoe, but you must take the greatest care, my dear, or you'll be terribly hurt.' He gazed upon her much as her own father would, proud but worried.

'Can there be any worse pain than what's tearing me apart now? If there is, it's a risk I'm prepared to take. No one has a greater right to make that mistake. Now it's up to me.'

He gave up the fight to dissuade her with a good grace. However much he disagreed with her plans, he knew well enough that he had lost the right to stop her when Ross failed to recognise her.

They walked back to the main complex together. Outside the building John took her hand and cradled it between his, subjecting her to a minute inspection.

'I'm glad to see you looking better, my dear. Try not to rush things too much. You'll do little good by knocking yourself out. I'll keep my fingers crossed that you'll soon be sending me some good news.' As he finished speaking his attention was distracted, and he looked away beyond her shoulder, raising a hand in greeting to someone out of her vision. 'Ah, there's Ross.'

Zoe's fingers closed tightly about his, drawing his frowning attention. 'You would tell me, wouldn't you, if

Ross isn't well? I can't help worrying. They haven't told you not to? My memories . . .'

'They, as you so aptly describe them, know nothing of our agreement. If there was anything for you to know, I would tell you. You can stop worrying. You must take care of yourself, my dear.'

Zoe nodded. Conscious of the man watching them, she let him go. 'You'd better go and see Ross.'

John smiled, tipping his head in acknowledgement, then he walked to where Ross waited for him. They disappeared, leaving Zoe feeling flat. Talking over the old wounds only made it clearer how hard her struggle was going to be. What she needed was some lively company to take her out of herself, because sometimes the line between despair and self-pity seemed awfully thin. She sought out Marian and they spent the rest of the afternoon on the beach with some of the other off-duty staff.

It was with a mixture of anticipation and trepidation that she made her preparations for dinner with Ross. Would he be the mocking stranger of a week ago, or would yesterday's mood, with all its promise, have carried over into today?

She was feeling distinctly nervous when she sat down before her dressing-table to apply a light make-up. A dusting of silvery-grey eye-shadow deepened her eyes into topaz pools, and a deft application of mascara and kohl gave them a distinctly exotic look. Just a shimmer of highlighter along her cheekbones accentuated the golden tan she had acquired during her stay, and she outlined the fullness of her lips in dusky rose. The effect, even she had to admit, was stunning.

She still had to decide what to wear, and time was running short. She could hardly go as she was, dressed only in a pair of lacy panties. She caught sight of herself in her mirror and wished, not for the first time, that she was less top-heavy. Then her eyes sought their mirror-image, and she knew what thoughts were hidden there.

Last year Ross had liked her just the way she was. She recalled the times when her body had been tuned to a wild response by the masterful caresses of the man she loved. Then her breasts had not been too full, nor her hips too curvaceous, but just hand-sized for the man who had brought her to full consciousness of herself as a woman. She had taken pride in the way he had made her feel, and the way she had been able to affect him in her turn. There had been no moments of insecurity during the whole of their time together.

With a sinking sensation in her stomach, Zoe knew she needed to feel the same way now. Surely it wasn't impossible to have it all again? She had so much love to give, physically and spiritually, and it was all having to be locked away inside her. She had the desperate feeling that if something did not happen very soon, she would explode like a bomb, destroying herself.

She gave herself a mental shake, studying the contents of her wardrobe with a jaundiced eye. Why was it that when forced to make a choice, she actively started to dislike every outfit she possessed? Finally she came back to one of her first choices and stepped into black silk trousers, and a camisole top with tiny buttons and thin straps. Gold-toned sandals and evening purse completed the outfit.

Yet it needed something to alleviate the plainness. She flicked open her jewellery box and extracted a chunky gold necklace which she fastened about her neck. About to close the lid, her eye was caught by the glint of red velvet, and after only the briefest of hesitations, Zoe removed the small square box and eased open the lid.

She eyed the sole occupant gravely, watching the light

catch the facets of the diamond cluster, each flash of fire tightening an invisible band around her heart. She touched a fingertip to the uneven surface and stroked it, smiling mistily as the memories came rushing back. So many of them were bittersweet now, but they were all she had—maybe all she would ever have.

The bemused jeweller had found them on his doorstep that morning, waiting for him to open up, both of them in evening dress. Ross had laughed and insisted she wear the ring. He wanted everybody to know they belonged to each other. They had been so in love it never occurred to them that they might only have a few more days together.

There was no struggle about whether to wear the ring or not—she had always known she would. She slipped it on to her right hand and eased the unfamiliar weight. It didn't feel right, the fit was looser, but it was preferable to not wearing it at all.

Ross arrived as she was spraying her favourite Givenchy perfume on her pulse spots. Suddenly she didn't feel at all like a twenty-three-year-old woman, but more like a naïve teenager. Her heart started drumming away fit to burst, and when she opened the door and saw him framed in the doorway, it did a sort of double flip and belly-flopped with a lurch.

He looked—her eyes skittered from his head to his heels—as if he had been poured into the white trousers, navy silk shirt and white jacket he was wearing. He fairly oozed with a magnetism so potent that it would have taken a superwoman to withstand it. Zoe was a mere woman. Her senses caught full force the bombardment of his rugged attraction and surrendered, completely overwhelmed. When Ross smiled, that old remembered bone-melting warmth invaded her limbs.

Her eyes scanned his face, searching for signs as to

which Ross she had to contend with. His smile was genuine pleasure and his eyes ... Zoe swallowed hastily, for his eyes held a depth and warmth of expression she had so longed to see reflected there for her. It was going to be all right, it just had to be. Somehow, somewhere, she must be doing something right, and whatever it was, she had to keep on doing it until everything came right again.

Only when he raised a hand and trailed one finger along her full lower lip in a caress that bordered on total possession did her own gasp bring her back to awareness. A tide of colour welled up in her cheeks and she took a step backward, gaining her equilibrium but losing his tantalising touch.

'You look ravishing,' Ross complimented her, his voice low and resonant. 'A blonde in black—the stuff dreams are made of.'

She smiled a little shyly into his amazingly tender eyes. 'Well, you mustn't fall asleep.'

He chuckled, lighting up his face. 'Oh, I don't think there's much chance of that. Shall we go?'

Zoe collected her purse. 'Don't you want me to tell you how you look?' she teased.

Ross ushered her out of the door. 'Your eyes already told me,' he countered, and Zoe was glad her back was to him to hide her blush.

They were expected at the Terrace restaurant, and were shown to a table overlooking the bay, but secluded by a wall of greenery. Most of the other diners recognised both Ross and herself, and Zoe could feel their speculative gazes upon her back as she made her way between the tables. It was a relief to slip into her seat and take refuge behind the wall of leaves.

Ross ordered their drinks, a dry martini for her and a whisky sour for himself, before sitting back and allowing his eyes to run over her again.

'I must admit to being intrigued. You give the outward impression of being an angel, yet I have a very vivid picture of you to the contrary.'

Zoe had the sinking feeling she was never going to live down that awful mistake with her bikini. She took a reviving sip of her martini. 'Unfair! I've already explained I had no idea I was showing ... that is, that my bikini was ...' She faltered to a halt, mostly because Ross was watching her intently over the rim of his glass, and it was plain that his mind's eye was seeing a picture of her that he had no intention of relinquishing.

His amused emerald gaze caressed her face. 'Maybe you did, maybe you didn't,' he continued aggravatingly to her dismay.

'Why can't you drop the subject? Its too embarrassing,' Zoe was finally goaded into answering, but she kept her gaze lowered on the glass she twirled between her fingers.

Ross reached out and stilled the movement, holding her hand loosely in his and rubbing his thumb caressingly over the tender skin of her palm. 'Even if I tell you it was one of the most beautiful sights I've ever seen?'

Zoe's lips formed a perfect O of surprise, although no sound found its way from her throat. It wasn't fair. He didn't need to try so hard to unsettle her by saying outrageous things. The mere presence of him had the same result. If only she could be sure of having the same devastating effect upon Ross.

'Have I suddenly grown another head?' Ross's laughing comment drew her attention with a start. 'You were staring. Didn't your mother ever tell you it was rude?'

'Yes, more than once. It must be your fatal charm that made me forget,' she flirted lightly, feeling rather strange and floaty inside.

'Oh, I have some charm then?' he teased with a rakish smile.

Zoe's own smile swept across her face. 'Oodles, when you care to show it to me, damn it!'

His answering grin was appreciative. 'You're hardly a calming influence yourself, dear Zoe,' he reminded her.

'Phooey!' she rejected his claim, but her pulse started a rapid tattoo at the way he said her name. Not the mocking honey or darling he had used. 'You're one of the biggest teases I know, so you can hardly expect me to believe that.'

Ross's teeth gleamed white in the low lighting. 'So you think I'm lying, do you?' Without another word he twisted her fingers from inside his palm until they were resting on the pulse at his wrist. The quickened beat told its own story beneath her sensitive touch. There was no way he could fake such testimony and Zoe swallowed convulsively as she raised her eyes to his.

The banked fires in his eyes were echoed in the husky note when he spoke. 'I think we'd better order before we forget what we're here for.'

'Yes,' Zoe breathed, still wrapped in his spell.

'Is that yes to food or to—something else?'

Zoe's smile was secretive, and she cast him a look from beneath her lashes. All she said in reply was a soft, 'Ah.' She retrieved her hand and added, 'May I see the menu, please.'

'Chicken,' Ross taunted, handing it to her.

'No, merely practical. If I don't eat now I'll have indigestion when I go to work.'

'Hm.' Ross bent his head over his own menu, 'I'll agree you need feeding,' he replied drolly.

Zoe's suspicions were aroused. 'Oh yes?'

Ross leant towards her conspiratorially. 'Because kittens who start spitting and clawing are known to purr when well fed. Shall I order for you?' He sat back at her indignant expression, his laugh full of satisfaction.

Excitement tightened knots in Zoe's stomach. When Ross set out to be charming and seductive, she knew of no equal. And of course, he would choose the most exotic and sensuous dishes for her to eat, so that all her senses would be focused on him. Which they were already, did he but know it. He must believe the chances of her giving in to his seduction were high, and not without reason. But he needn't think he could win her over so easily. Yet eating a meal wasn't consenting to anything, so why not?

Zoe snapped the card shut decisively and held it out to him. 'Very well, you choose. It should be an education.'

Ross held her gaze, acknowledging her challenge with admiration in his eyes. 'Here begins the first lesson. I can hardly wait for graduation.'

Zoe raised finely arched brows. 'School might not be all it's cracked up to be,' she flirted dangerously.

His lips twitched but he replied solemnly, 'Only if the teacher is a bad one. I have every confidence in my ability to ... satisfy the needs of my pupil.'

Her pulse was rioting haphazardly, but she couldn't let that go by without an answer. 'Actions speak louder than words. A fool can speak a great deal and say absolutely nothing.'

Ross tipped his head, conceding the point. 'Touché,' was all he said, but his eyes held promises.

The food when it arrived was delicious. They dined on avocados stuffed with cream cheese and chives, fresh lobster, and ice-cream made from coconuts. Coffee and liqueurs rounded off the meal perfectly, and Zoe sat back in her seat with a sigh of pleasure.

'Good food is one of the most satisfying experiences in the world,' she pronounced, licking her lips in remembrance.

She watched Ross raise his glass to her before taking an appreciative sip. All the while his gaze never left her, and he seemed to be savouring the essence of her as he rolled the liquid across his tongue. It was a highly charged moment, with an eroticism that awakened her body instantly. That he had no need to touch her to have her breasts quickening, thrusting her nipples against the fragile material of her top, and starting the throbbing ache in the pit of her stomach, was a revelation. She had forgotten what it could be like, this all-consuming wave of desire.

'After making love,' he agreed softly.

The pictures his statement conjured up made the sensitive hairs of her body stand on end. 'I didn't say that.'

'You didn't need to. You're a sensualist. I could tell the second you began to sing, and the most sensual experience you can know is to make love. Only then do we use all our senses.'

He was doing it again, building mental pictures that could set her alight. She tried to think of something to say to lower her temperature and divert him into less emotive channels, but wasn't given the chance.

Ross leant across and took her hand, refusing to allow her to pull away. 'Does it embarrass you to talk about sex?'

A small gasp left her. 'I didn't know we were discussing sex. I was under the impression we were talking of making love!' she corrected, sensing a subtle change in the atmosphere, making her feel uneasy.

There was a tightening about his lips and eyes as he

gave her his full attention. 'Ah! So you believe there's a distinction between the two.' There was a strange note in his voice she was at a loss to interpret.

'Of course there is, and you know it,' she argued hotly.

Ross shook his head. He was not looking at her so much as a point in the middle distance beyond her shoulder. Idly he began to twist the ring she wore between his fingers. 'Do I? I may have believed I did in my ignorance.' His laugh was bitter. 'But not any more.' With a shake of the head he dismissed his odd mood and focused on the hand he held. 'A beautiful ring. From a rich admirer?'

Zoe could feel her colour draining away. God, how that hurt. It took every ounce of willpower to keep the evidence of it from her expressive face. She felt choked, and a tidal wave of sorrow at the bitter irony made her eyes glitter like fool's gold. 'No,' she answered, and her voice wobbled. 'Someone I love and respect very much gave it to me, and if you don't mind I'd rather not talk about it just now.'

He watched her for long minutes, the mocking words that should have followed her declaration being held back at the sound of her obvious distress. His unexpected consideration choked her up again. Ross released her hand with an apologetic smile. 'Forgive me. I had no idea I was—intruding.'

Intruding? Oh, God, if only he knew. If only she dared tell him!

'It appears we're both walking wounded,' he declared with what sounded suspiciously like sympathy.

'Yes, in a way,' Zoe agreed, smiling faintly. 'Only I haven't given up on love, like you.'

'That's the difference between a fool and a wise man,' he drawled with heavy irony.

Zoe didn't need to ask who was the fool in his opinion.

Maybe he would be proved right one day, but she sincerely hoped not. Despite her words to John Vernon, she knew to lose Ross for a second time would be a heavy cross to bear. So she had to keep believing his love wasn't dead, only missing. That one day it would come back to life and prove her faith was justified.

'You've gone very quiet.' Ross's voice broke into her thoughts, making her start. When she met his eyes she saw at once he had shaken off his own introspection.

Her movements were jerky and her laugh was more off-key than off-hand. 'I was just indulging in a spot of wishful thinking.'

'Mm, so was I.' Ross's eyes tracing their velvet way over her face and down to where her breasts still thrust against the skimpy material left her in little doubt as to what his thoughts had been.

She resisted the anxious urge to cross her arms over her chest, and stared him out. Finally, with a half laugh, Ross raised a hand to concede the point to her.

'OK, OK, I get the message.' He saw a flicker of surprise in her eyes and raised an eyebrow. 'Or do I? You're a bit of a puzzle, Zoe Winthrop, a living, breathing contradiction. Sometimes you appear too vulnerable to be in the cut-and-thrust world of entertainment. What made you take it up?'

This was safer ground for Zoe. She relaxed muscles she hadn't realised were stretched taut. 'Actually there was very little doubt about what I would do with my life. My father had his own jazz band and my mother used to sing with them. They run their own club in London. As I grew older I started to sing there too. Not that they pushed me, one way or the other, but I love to sing, and people enjoy listening to me. I was lucky. It all came together for me.'

'Very impressive. I know myself how talented you are.

I hear nothing but praise for you from all sides. What made you leave home and come to Mariposa?'

The question opened the door for Zoe, if she cared to take it. Maybe a word could jog his memory. She watched him carefully through her lashes, not wanting to miss any change in his expression—if there should be one. 'Last year I spent my holiday at your hotel on Crete. I saw you there, but I don't suppose you'd remember me among all the other guests.'

His interest sharpened, and he sat forward, eyes narrowing. 'What time of year was this?'

Zoe licked her lips nervously. 'Late summer.'

A harsh laugh was his response as he sat back again, but his eyes were angry. 'That would explain it. If I saw you I wouldn't remember. In fact, I can't remember anything about that time at all.' He laughed again, but there was little of humour in it and a lot of bitter anger and frustration. Then a thought struck him and he eyed her fixedly. 'If you saw me there, you must have seen who I was with. Did you?'

Lord, how to answer that! 'I ... didn't take much notice, I'm afraid.'

'Damn it!'

Compassion filled her. 'Ross, it will come one day.'

He looked furious. 'I'm up to here with platitudes, Zoe. The way you can help me is to tell me what you saw. Where I went, who I was with.'

'I can't,' she said huskily.

His gaze honed in. 'Why not? Were you lying to me? Do you know something? Hell, I've told you how I feel about my loss of memory. Now you sit there holding back!' Frustration and suspicion were rapidly gaining the upper hand.

Hastily Zoe found her voice. 'I'm not holding back. Believe me, if there was anything that I could tell you I would do so. I'm not able to.'

For several seconds he eyed her steadily, then with a visible effort he forced himself to relax. 'I'm sorry,' he apologised, 'I shouldn't get angry, I know. It's this damn brick wall in my head. If just once I could see a crack in it, a small glimmer of light in the darkness—but there's absolutely nothing. It remains inviolate. How the hell can I know the why, if I can't see the who and the where?'

Zoe frowned her confusion. 'Ross, you aren't making sense.'

'If I can't understand it, don't expect me to explain to you.' He mocked them both.

'You obviously have some suspicions,' Zoe began, shaking her head to clear away her own disappointment, trying to concentrate on his. 'Can't you tell me what they are? Maybe I could help a little.'

'They aren't suspicions, they're hard facts.'

He had lost her. 'You're talking about before the crash?'

'I'm talking about being taken for a fool. For letting oneself down.' He stopped abruptly and forced a smile to his lips. 'Forget it. Let's change the subject, shall we. You might mean well, but if you can't tell me anything, there's nothing more to be said.'

She wanted to protest, to make him go on until she knew what he meant, but she had no excuse for doing so. As before, the subject was closed. He had allowed her a tantalising glimpse of the confused man behind the mask, but that was all. Instead of helping to solve the mystery, it had served to pose another.

Zoe took a steadying breath, 'I'm sorry, I ...' She caught his look which told her plainly he neither wanted nor needed her sympathy, and changed tack. 'Anyway, I enjoyed myself on Crete, and when this vacancy arose I jumped at the chance of broadening my horizons.'

'And didn't your lover have anything to say about your sailing off across the Atlantic? Or is that what forced you apart, your longing for fame and the bright lights?'

There could be no mistaking the taunt in Ross's voice this time. As if aware he had revealed too much, he now advanced the battle into her court. She cursed her foolishness in bringing up the crash, for it was that which had reacted on him so badly. Yet it made her angry too, to realise how quickly he could start condemning her again.

Zoe took a careful sip of her drink, refusing to reply as angrily to his suggestion as she wanted to do. 'Must you always ask personal questions?'

Ross shrugged casually. 'It sounded a perfectly reasonable question to me.' Unfortunately he made no attempt to disguise the mocking glint in his eye.

Zoe gritted her teeth, barely able to contain her growing fury at his continual sniping. 'I hope you'll forgive me when I tell you to mind your own damn business!' she forced out icily.

'Then I'm right,' he confirmed with some satisfaction.

She wanted to cry. In a few short words she had lost all the ground she had won. 'You couldn't be further from the truth if you were standing on Pluto,' she stated coldly.

They stared each other out, she angry, he mocking, neither giving way, until Zoe could stand it no longer and closed her eyes.

Ross sighed wearily and her lids lifted, her eyes darting to his. He looked defeated and she didn't know what to make of it. 'It's getting late. We'd better go. Will you come back to the bungalow for coffee?'

Zoe looked hastily down at her hands. No apology, just dismissal. What a mess. How had everything gone so disastrously wrong? If she had any sense she would refuse his offer. He had upset her and made her angry, but there was no denying she still felt more alive with him than without him. If she wanted to spend time with him, she had to accept him as he was, because she was beginning to think he would never change. So she lifted her head and nodded.

She allowed him to help her to her feet and accepted his arm as he guided her from the restaurant and down to the moonlit path through the grounds. Ross walked stiffly beside her, an invisible wall holding them emotionally apart. Yet Zoe was vitally aware of the touch of Ross's hand on her arm, creating a disturbing warmth that ran through her like quicksilver. Eventually Ross slowed his step to match her shorter one, and at the same time Zoe was aware of a softening of his rigid frame. Every now and again their thighs brushed as they walked, sending an electric current of awareness into the air around them.

She wasn't surprised when he halted in the shadow of a tree, but she was when he gave a deep sigh and took her shoulders between his hands, starting up fires where he ran them up and down her soft skin.

'I'm sorry, Zoe. I promised myself I wouldn't start accusing you unfairly again, when I know none of it is your fault. I thought I was doing quite well, but talking about Crete made me see red, I'm afraid. You don't have to tell me I hurt you, I could see that for myself. All I can say is, I didn't want to do it but I couldn't help myself. Do you believe me?'

She really hadn't been expecting this, but the sincerity in his voice couldn't be denied. He was trying to put things right and she couldn't ignore one of the few conciliatory gestures he had made.

'Yes, I believe you,' she whispered, feeling choked. She could understand what made him act as he had, even if the details were denied her. All she wanted to do was help him forget the bad times so that they could share the good. She could stand a little hurt to achieve that. He wasn't to know how deep her wounds were.

She watched him smile as he reached out and drew her to him, his sensitive hands sliding around her waist and down to her hips to pull her heart-stoppingly close to the warmth and strength of his body. For one awful second it crossed her mind that he had apologised solely because it was doubtful if she would have gone so willingly into his arms if he hadn't. Then she dismissed it as unworthy. He would never stoop that low. Her hands steadied on his arms as she leant back slightly to look up at him.

She could sense the wry grimace on his lips as he said, 'All I seem to be doing is apologising to you. You take all I dish out and come back for more, without understanding any of it.'

'I want you to tell me,' she breathed truthfully, 'but I can wait until you're ready.' Hadn't she been doing just that?

'That might be never,' he warned, just as softly as she.

She shrugged, ignoring that that was what she was afraid of. 'There's nowhere I have to go in a hurry.'

'Don't expect miracles, Zoe, I've stopped believing in them.'

Didn't she know that feeling? 'Me too. It was a salutary lesson I'll never forget. Now I live from day to day. No ties, no promises.' It wasn't true but it was what he wanted to hear.

'We think alike, you and I. Who would have thought I would find a girl like you here? Hell, I thought it was going to be dull.' His head dipped until their lips were only a sigh apart. 'Beautiful Zoe, I've wanted this moment since I saw you tonight. God knows how I had the patience to keep my hands off you,' he growled huskily.

Zoe's fingers tightened on his arms, feeling the tension building in him. 'They say its good for the soul, patience,' she teased, darting out her tongue to moisten lips gone suddenly dry.

Ross groaned as the pink tip disappeared. 'My soul may be satisfied but my body hungers for you. Kiss me, Zoe.'

His command was gruff, but his lips were a gentle caress as they finally possessed hers. Zoe shut out the world and opened her heart to him. The feel of the warm male lips opening over hers, coaxing her into welcoming his invasion, while his hands closed her yet more firmly against the stirring of his own thighs, brought a moan from deep in her throat.

It was as if that was the signal he had been waiting for. In an instant what had started out as a search became a passionate demand that she responded to blindly. Her arms slid up to tighten about his neck, pressing herself to him. She met the probing seduction of his tongue with her own, spiralling out of control on a hot tide of wanting. Each time he kissed her the need grew worse, her response that much more abandoned. When Ross moved his body against her in frustrated imitation of his own desire, flames overwhelmed her. His hand found its way beneath her silky top and began tracing its way along the sensitised skin of her back, and all she could think of was the intensity of her wish to have that touch on her breasts.

When her legs threatened to support her no longer, Ross leant back against the tree and drew her between his thighs until not a breath of air could pass between their locked bodies. He groaned, his hands spanning her ribs, gliding upwards, his thumbs grazing the rise of her breasts, pushing the soft material on her top away to bare her heated skin to the balmy breezes. Zoe felt as if she was floating dizzily on a mindless sea, rocked by the sudden assault of desire and need. She forgot his mocking words, forgot everything but that she loved him and wanted him, and that he was here with her now.

In another second she would be begging him to ease the congested ache of her flesh, and it was this more than anything that brought back a measure of sanity. The leap into passion was shocking in its intensity, and though she craved appeasement, her mind warned her it was too soon. With a sob she dragged her mouth from his, momentarily bereft at the cessation of the life-giving contact, then she buried her head in the curve of his shoulder, her whole body quivering.

Ross's breathing echoed raggedly in her ear, steadying slowly as he dragged fresh air into his lungs. The tension of his body matched hers, relaxing only by sheer effort of will. At last he moved, his hands going to her shoulders, holding her at arm's length.

'That was more than I bargained for. I thought I had more control. I had an idea we'd be good together, but not that we'd both go up like dry tinder. Do you want me to apologise, Zoe?' There was more than a hint of a laugh in his voice as he finished.

Zoe moved her hands to rest against the silk of his shirt, unconsciously tracing the hard planes of his chest beneath the thin covering, finding the male nipples and running her fingers around them until he drew a sharp breath. She laughed a little too. 'No. I was taken by surprise too. I thought I could handle it. I should have known.' Should have remembered that she and Ross had always been a combustible combination.

Ross pulled her close again for a brief moment that ended much too soon. 'Me too. But that was something else.' He sounded a little shaken, as well he might. His body remembered even if he did not, but it remembered her from where they had left off, not the beginning, where Ross's mind was now. 'I think we both need a strong cup of coffee, don't you?' He turned her in the direction of his bungalow, and with one arm still about her, they moved on. It was a strange moment, with Ross making a determined effort to lighten the atmosphere and give them both a breathing space.

'You know, that coffee was only a ploy to get you into my clutches, but I'm damned if I don't actually need it now.' Ross's confession was wry.

'Well, it serves you right for plotting against me.' She laughed unsympathetically, while admitting to herself that she felt the same. It was confusing to have gone so wildly out of control this time, when he had kissed her before. Why not then? She knew the answer to that. It was his attitude which had made her hold back that little bit that she had relinquished tonight. Only she had come to her senses before she had told him she loved him. That would have been fatal.

They climbed the steps of the bungalow and their footsteps echoed on the wooden boards of the veranda. In the pool of light cast by the lamp left burning in the lounge, Ross paused to look down at her.

'You could turn out to be a very dangerous lady.'

Zoe tried to learn something from his face, but he had his back to the light and remained shadowed. She was forced to ask, 'Is that good or bad?'

'I think I'll reserve judgement.' His reply was cautious, then he laughed outright. 'After all, you're good, but when you're bad you could be better.'

Zoe afforded him an old-fashioned look, but couldn't

hold back a laugh, not so much at what he said, but that he said it with genuine humour.

'Coffee,' she reminded him reprovingly.

'Coffee,' he agreed soberly, and within a very short space of time they were seated in his lounge, sipping steaming cups of the aromatic brew.

'I didn't know you were acquainted with John Vernon.' Ross's remark came totally out of the blue.

Zoe's tongue actually felt as if it were stuck to the roof of her mouth, and she was glad she still had some coffee left to lubricate it. Unfortunately her brain had seized up too.

'Wh . . . who did you say?' she improvised somewhat less than brilliantly.

Ross looked at her oddly and Zoe couldn't say she was altogether surprised. 'John Vernon,' he repeated carefully, then added, 'the man you were talking to this afternoon.'

'Oh, him! Why, did he mention me?' Damn, but she sounded far too guilty for such an innocent comment.

There was a short silence before Ross went on blandly. 'Nary a word, but you know I saw you together and you seemed friendly enough. I wasn't accusing you of seeing another man, Zoe. Apart from anything else, I don't have the right. It did occur to me that you might know John in a professional capacity. If you're not well I would want to know, as your employer and on a personal level.'

It did her heart good to hear him say what he did, but she wondered what he would say if she told him he did have the right he denied. Caution prevailed. 'Actually we are slightly acquainted. I did consult him at one time but I'm quite well now. I was very surprised to find him here.' Was there ever a greater understatement?

'What was wrong with you?'

Zoe took another sip of coffee, her mind working furiously. Finally she managed to hedge, 'I ... I had been in an accident, and with certain injuries you have to be careful. Fortunately for me there was nothing serious.'

'But the memories aren't good?'

'No, they're not good,' she agreed flatly.

Ross's full lips twisted into a grimace. 'At least you can remember that. Whereas I ...' he stopped short.

Zoe held her breath, hoping against hope that he was going to tell her what had happened to him, but it wasn't to be. Instead he spoke of something else altogether.

'I'll be busy tomorrow, so I won't be seeing you, but on Sunday I thought you might enjoy a trip round the island. How does that appeal to you?'

Zoe tried to hide the tell-tale signs of just how much it appealed. 'I'd like that. I always wanted to see more of the island.'

One eyebrow rose. 'If I come too, it won't spoil your enjoyment at all?'

She grinned. 'Oh, I think I could stand it.'

'Your mother must have had the devil of a time with you,' Ross growled.

'But she loved me.' Zoe began to laugh.

'Hmn, I'm beginning to see why,' he declared thoughtfully, and Zoe had the greatest difficulty controlling her breathing. Don't read too much into it, she warned herself, but it was hard, very hard, not to.

Much later, when he walked her back to the nightclub, Ross contented himself with pressing a gentle kiss on her lips. 'Until Sunday,' he murmured, accompanying the words with a smile that took her breath away.

Zoe recalled the moment again as she lay on a lounger outside her chalet the following afternoon. She grinned

at the whimsical thought that she wouldn't mind going
permanently breathless if Ross would only keep on
looking at her the way he had last night. This led her on
to daydreaming about a bright future where nothing
from the past could hurt them. That was probably why
Marian Ritchie's news affected her the way it did.

The little brunette came by for coffee and a chat and
set in motion a chain reaction which hit Zoe at the most
primitive level, revealing her insecurity in a waking
nightmare. All Marian had time to say was that
strangers, a man and a woman, had arrived by boat and
Ross had left the island with them.

Zoe's reaction was unequivocal. Her mind leapt back
to that other time, and she panicked, startling her friend
completely by jumping up from the lounger and rushing
off along the track through the trees. She came to an
abrupt halt at the edge of the clearing, studying the
shuttered and silent bungalow through eyes that
sparkled with unshed tears. Logic and common sense
departed and a sickening feeling of *déjà vu* made her
sway dizzily.

All that registered was that Ross had gone—and the
fear, that somehow his parents had learned she was here
and had spirited Ross away. And it wasn't fair. Didn't
they have any pity at all? What they had said to her
before, when she had been still unwell herself, had been
nothing short of sadistic. Hadn't she suffered enough?
She had done all that was asked of her and more, and still
they sought to hound her.

Zoe shuddered, caught in the grip of a remembered
pain that had the power to destroy her. She thought she
had grown stronger, able to withstand the knocks that
life was throwing her, but all that she had managed to do
was leave herself wide open and vulnerable.

Her memories took over until they were passing

before her eyes, blanking out the beauty before her. She couldn't seem to still the shaking inside her. Unable to stop it, the past ran through her mind like a film run at the wrong speed. She could only remember.

She had met Ross at precisely seventeen minutes past two on a hot Cretan afternoon. She recalled that with complete accuracy, for she had been looking at her watch when she walked straight into him. She had a tour coach to catch and she was running late, when she walked into the lift and into Ross Lyneham's arms, and her life was never the same again.

Whatever special magic there was that had invaded her at his innocently steadying touch had worked on him too. By the time the lift reached the ground floor, he had invited her to join him for coffee and she had accepted.

He was the most attractive man she had ever met, and she had met her share. None of her previous experience had prepared her for the impact of this man. She hadn't been able to take her eyes off him. Her senses were stunned by the way he moved and the sound of his voice. The incredible thing was that she didn't feel in the least embarrassed by the way she was acting, nor by the way he was reacting to her. It had been amazingly, totally, right.

Yet during all the following week, he had barely touched her, except to hold her hand while they walked and talked. He didn't try to seduce her, to take advantage of the open attraction she felt for him. Talking was what they did most of. They didn't seem able to stop once they got started, for it was incredible just how much they discovered they had in common. It became a contest to find out what they didn't like. Ross hated Rachmaninov, crime novels and gooey cakes, while Zoe loathed Mahler, science fiction and Fisher-man's Friends. Which left them with a shared interest in most sports, books and music, and a mutual passion for sailing, swimming and walking.

She hadn't, at first, known who he was. Ross had told her his name, but it meant nothing to her. She simply assumed that, like her, he was on holiday. When he finally told her he owned the hotel chain, plus many other interests worldwide, she had been shocked into speechlessness, and when, in the silence, he went on to explain why he had been so reserved, she saw that he had actually been apprehensive about telling her. Immediately she had understood why. All his adult life he had been sought after by women, and gradually over the years he had come cynically to understand that, while he was enormously attractive as a man, the attraction was greatly improved by the fact that he was the possessor of such wealth and power.

Not unnaturally, he had come to suspect a woman's motives. As a rule his emotions were never seriously under assault, so that this time he had surprised himself by the depth of his own response, so much so that a degree of uncertainty had crept into his mind. It produced a vulnerability that he hadn't experienced since his youth when he had first become the victim of one of society's predatory females.

Zoe's surprise at his confession did much to persuade him that her feelings were genuinely for the man he was and not the tycoon. Not that he was that easy to convince. She worked desperately hard to dismiss his doubts, but they couldn't all be wiped out by a few words. So much depended on trust, and that could only come with time.

Strangely, even when she discovered who he was and how he felt, the relationship stayed unchanged. That didn't mean there was no physical attraction. That vital ingredient had been there from the beginning. But it seemed more important to get to know each other than to satisfy the excitement that ran back and forth between them. Ross joked a lot about nobody believing him if he told them that he had spent so much time with a beautiful woman without so much as kissing her, but Zoe recognised the sadness in that. It hadn't taken her long to realise that there was more to him than the image he had chosen to project. He was caring and compassionate, loving and teasing, a whole complexity of things that he never showed to the world because, for the most part, they were only interested in the wealthy businessman he was. He showed her another side, the side she fell in love with, but it was the complete man that she came to love—businessman and man.

Only then, when the time was right, did the relationship deepen. It was love that made their coming together so perfect and right. For a few glorious weeks they shared the wonder of exploration. By day the island, and by night the island that was their love.

She didn't know, then, how short their time together was going to be.

They danced for hours the night Ross asked her to marry him. Much later they sat on the beach watching the sun come up, because sleeping meant ending the day, and they wanted it to last for ever. Ross bought her a ring as soon as the jewellers opened for business, a beautiful diamond cluster that caught the sunlight and shot rainbow sparks.

Two days later they flew to America to tell his parents the news, intending to travel on to England afterwards. For some reason Zoe never discovered, their flight was diverted south. It had been her idea to take the train to New York. It had sounded romantic to book a first-class compartment, but it hadn't been like that. Six hours out, the lead carriages were derailed and she was plunged into a dark pit of pain and terror, emerging at last to discover that what had seemed a nightmare was stark reality.

Her injuries, compared with those unfortunate souls who had not survived, were light. A cracked rib, a broken arm and multiple cuts and bruises. Blessedly she didn't remember at first what had happened, they kept her heavily sedated to ease the pain in her chest because breathing was agony. But there came a time when there was no cocooning, and she recalled clearly her last sight of Ross, smiling at her from the far end of the club car.

She had been laughing at him because he had been buttonholed by the proverbial travelling salesman, when the sudden impact had flung her violently backwards. The hand she threw out to save herself had smacked into the wall and the blinding pain had made her scream. All about her was a tumbling, crying body of people and the piercing shriek of tortured metal. Then came the terrifying sensation of falling, rolling. Zoe was thrown against something hard and sharp and knew no more, until she awoke in a hospital bed days later.

The worst was yet to come. Nobody seemed to know or have heard of Ross. Zoe became hysterical, trying to get out of bed, thrusting away the nurses who tried to stop her, and in the end they had to sedate her again. When next she came round they tried to explain to her that the victims had been split between three hospitals and that it was quite possible the man she sought was at one of the others. She didn't believe them, convinced they were waiting until she was strong enough to take it to tell her he was dead.

It took the words of three nurses, individually and together, to convince her when they finally located Ross in another hospital. He was seriously ill, but hanging on. She managed to get infrequent reports via a friendly nurse who had connections with the other hospital, but as the days passed and the reports showed very little improvement, the strain began seriously to affect her own recovery.

Her nights were constantly racked by nightmares, and not being able to see Ross for herself did not help. She forced herself to be cheerful when she called her parents to reassure them that she was recovering, but even so they had been so shocked by the news of her accident that they would have flown out to see for themselves. Only at Zoe's insistence did they agree not to come, and she realised why they had given in so easily when her cousin Elizabeth had arrived from Canada the very next day.

The day she was discharged she persuaded Elizabeth to drive her to Mercy Hospital. Ross had been moved into a private room, so her informant had said, and Zoe had been approaching the door when it opened and a man and woman emerged. She had known at once who they were. The similarity between Ross and his father was striking, only this man was older and harder. The woman at his side was coldly beautiful and elegant, not a hair out of place.

And they disliked her.

They watched her walking towards them as if she were some lower form of life which had just crawled out from under a stone. Zoe felt the first moment of unease then, but they were Ross's parents and whatever they were like, they would be as worried as she was, so she owed them consideration. Already nervous and sick with apprehension, nevertheless she managed to fix a tiny smile on her face as greeting.

'You have to be Ross's parents. Tell me, how is he?' She held out her hand, but when neither offered to return the gesture she dropped it to her side, a wave of humiliated colour staining her cheeks.

His mother looked her up and down. 'And you are?'

Zoe was rather taken aback, 'I'm Zoe Winthrop, I . . .'

'I suppose you're one of Ross's—women. He never did show much taste. What do you do?'

Zoe frowned in dismay. 'Why . . . I . . . I'm a singer.' she managed to stutter out. Never had she been spoken to in such a way.

The couple exchanged a look, then his father spoke for the first time. 'Our son is not to be disturbed. I'll thank you to keep away. Come along, Deirdre.'

Zoe quickly stepped in front of them to halt their departure. 'Oh, but you don't understand. I'm Ross's fiancée. We're to be married. I have a right to know how he is.'

His mother's voice dropped a couple of icy degrees, 'You jest, of course. My son would never agree to marry a common singer.'

For a minute Zoe didn't know what to say. She was already feeling the strain of her first day out of hospital, and to meet and fight such an attitude was almost beyond her. 'If you don't believe me, ask Ross,' she finally uttered unsteadily.

His father gripped her shoulder and manhandled her out of the way, 'This conversation has gone on long enough. My son is in a coma. Even had he not been we would hardly need to ask him, we know the answer. Kindly take yourself back to wherever it was you came from.'

Zoe only heard the first half of his speech. 'In a coma?' she blanched and swayed on her suddenly weak legs. 'Oh my God! I must see him. He needs me.'

'You can stop right there, young lady.' His father held her again to halt her instinctive move towards the door which hid Ross from her sight. 'You aren't going within a country mile of our son. You may think you're on to a lucrative scheme but you're mistaken.'

'You don't understand. I love Ross. He loves me. We're engaged to be married. I have the right to see him,' Zoe insisted, but her voice grew fainter at the uncompromising looks on both their faces.

His mother was unmoved by the visible signs of distress on the younger woman's face. 'This is a disgusting exhibition. Do something, Cole. I will not have this—person—visiting my son.'

Zoe's scanty hold on her frayed nerves snapped at that description, 'Oh don't be such a fool, you stupid woman! I won't hurt him, I can help him.'

Cole Lyneham had no compunction about slapping her face. 'That is quite enough.'

She reeled back against the opposite wall at the force of the blow, her hand automatically rising to cover the spot. She stared at them both in dawning horror—they weren't going to let her see him under any circumstances. Zoe made a desperate lunge for the door and had even managed to open it when rough hands pulled her forcibly away.

Almost immediately they were surrounded by people, nurses and doctors mingling with inquisitive visitors. In a dream she heard his father order the staff not to let her in to see Ross or to have any communication with her. She cried out against the injustice of it, but in vain.

She was too distraught to do more than let a pair of gentle hands usher her away. They turned out to belong to John Vernon, a specialist who had been called in at Ross's parents' request. He took her away and listened to her story and never for one moment doubted the truth of it. He became her friend and confidante. During the first months he kept her well informed of Ross's progress, but when it became clear, once he roused from the coma, that Ross was suffering from a form of amnesia, John advised Zoe to return to England.

There was little else she could do. Barred from seeing Ross herself, the anguished waiting was only upsetting her more. There was nothing to be done until Ross's memory returned. John promised to keep her well informed and this he did, but long months passed without change. Then suddenly Ross was once again in the news, the darling of New York society. Zoe was forced to witness his return to health through the media, and still he didn't remember. Resolutely she pushed to the back of her mind that perhaps he didn't want to. The Ross she loved would never do that. Never . . . never . . .

When Marian came up behind Zoe's rigid form and touched her arms, she was appalled by the trembling beneath her fingers. 'Zoe? For heaven's sake, what's the matter?'

Zoe moaned as her friend's voice intruded on her waking nightmare, and twisted round, still in a state of shock. 'Oh God!' she moaned.

Marian studied the shocked, white face and knew that if Zoe didn't sit down, she would fall down. Taking her by the arm, her voice was firm. 'Sit down Zoe,' she ordered, mightily relieved when she was obeyed. 'Now listen to me. Ross has gone to New Caledonia to play golf with friends. He'll be back tonight. Do you understand?'

Zoe heard her and felt faint with shock and relief. She turned a startled face to Marian then buried her head against her knees, feeling sick. 'Oh God, what a fool! How stupid, stupid!' Tears of pure relief racked her body. It was some time before she regained her control, and another few minutes before she felt competent enough to speak.

'I feel as if I've been through the wringer,' she sighed, drained by her emotional reaction. Tiredly she rested her head back against the tree behind her.

Marian chewed on a blade of grass, eyeing her with concern. 'I'm sorry, I didn't know.'

Too enervated to think properly yet, Zoe looked at her friend in confusion, 'About what?'

'That you loved him like that,' Marian explained with a directness that Zoe couldn't combat.

She stiffened automatically, for self-defence. 'I . . .' she began, only to stop. How did she explain away her behaviour?

Marian gave her a sideways look. 'You can deny it till the cows come home, but I won't believe you. You went into a flat spin, my girl.'

Zoe didn't know where to look, then she caught Marian's eyes and noted that whilst they were amused, they were also kindly. 'You must think I'm crazy.'

'Does anyone in love act totally sane? I never have.'

Zoe lowered her eyes to hide her expression. 'Yes, but I've only known Ross a matter of days.'

'What difference does that make? It's not how long you've known someone but the depth of feeling that counts.'

'You sound as if you speak from experience.' Zoe blinked at her.

'I haven't remained unscathed,' Marian admitted with a wry twist of her lips. 'I found it helped to talk things over. I'll listen if you want.'

Zoe took a deep breath, gratitude bringing a lump to her throat. 'Marian, I'd like nothing better, but I simply can't.'

Marian accepted that with a small shrug. 'It's not the end of the world, Zoe.'

The laugh that left Zoe at that statement was full of bitterness. 'If only you knew.'

Marian managed to hide her surprise. 'You were

knocked for a loop.'

Zoe sighed. 'I thought he'd gone, and I couldn't live with that. I've suffered that way once before.'

It was what she didn't say that made Marian take a quick look at Zoe's serious face. 'Were you very unhappy?'

Zoe couldn't have summoned a smile of denial even if she had wanted to. 'I've been so lonely,' she whispered, her voice catching on a sob.

'Oh, Zoe!' Marian's eyes were suddenly swamped with tears. That admission had been full of a pain too unbearable to contemplate. 'Tell me. Don't keep it to yourself,' she urged.

Zoe buried her head against her knees, 'I can't. I made a promise.'

'Who to?' The probe was gentle.

'A nest of vipers,' Zoe declared bitterly, scrubbing at her eyes. His family had demanded she did not contact Ross, an angry John Vernon had explained. She knew it was because they wanted nothing to do with her, but she agreed only because John had convinced her she might do him more harm than good.

Yet the true reason remained. She wasn't good enough for them. In her innocence she had imagined they would welcome her because of her relationship with their son. What a joke that had turned out to be. She had never in her life come up against people who could act that way. It was a lesson she was never likely to forget.

Zoe made a determined effort and pulled herself together. 'No more sympathy, please!' she begged Marian, her smile unforced. 'As you can see, I can't take it.'

Marian wiped her own eyes and accepted that Zoe wasn't about to say any more. 'I'm a bit watery myself. Must be the sun in my eyes.' Considering they were sitting in the shade, this made them both laugh.

Taking herself in hand, Zoe climbed to her feet and dusted herself down. 'I think I'll go for a walk. I need time to get myself together.'

Marian scrambled up too. 'OK, but if you want some company, just come over.'

Zoe nodded her thanks and walked away. She needed to think. Was she getting anywhere with Ross? He had been different the last few days, but was that a good enough reason to hope? Was she clinging too much to the past to be able to see the future clearly? She wished she knew. She wished Ross would tell her why he had changed so much. Somehow she knew it all hinged on this mysterious woman. Nothing could be settled until her ghost was laid. When would that be? This year, next year, some time . . . never?

There were only questions, no answers.

Zoe kept on walking.

CHAPTER FIVE

ZOE was already dressed, with a bikini beneath a towelling set of shorts and top in a cool shade of peach, when Ross arrived half an hour early on Sunday morning. His long athletic legs were emphasised by a disreputable pair of cut-off jeans for shorts, and a white vest set off the tanned muscular planes of his chest and arms. He had his towel draped about his neck and a pair of sunglasses dangled from the hand he had propped himself against the door jamb with. His eyes travelled over her appreciatively.

'Good, you're ready.' He levered himself upright, tucking his fingers into the pockets of his shorts. He looked more relaxed than she had seen him for a long time.

Zoe returned his look and knew the day would be fraught with temptation. He was altogether too potent. She felt a shiver of anticipation run through her.

'You look good enough to eat. Ripe and peachy,' he added, tormenting her with yet another examination.

Zoe did her best to look reproving. 'Just don't imagine I'm going to fall into your hands. Scrumping is not allowed.'

He laughed. 'Scrumping?'

'Stealing fruit from someone else's trees, as practised by small and grubby schoolboys,' she clarified, only to hear him laugh again.

'OK, no scrumping. But as I own the island, the trees already belong to me. So what does that make you?' There was a distinctly possessive note in his answer and

in the way he took her hand. The heat glowing behind
his emerald gaze rivalled the sun's rays on her skin.

It was one of those times when a really good answer
didn't spring to mind, and she was left having to pretend
his words hadn't had any effect whatsoever. 'Are we
going by boat?' she queried instead as they made their
way down to the beach.

'No. I thought we'd walk. It's not a very big island. Do
you mind?'

Zoe smiled. 'Oh, no. I enjoy walking.'

'Good,' he pronounced with satisfaction, 'that's
something we have in common.'

The irony of that made her smile to herself. If Ross
was frustrated by his lack of memory, then it was no
more than she, only she couldn't admit it. Talking to
Ross was like walking on eggshells.

They walked slowly, beachcombing as they went.
There was a warm breeze off the sea that cooled their
sun-kissed limbs and tugged at their hair as they
fossicked. Occasionally Ross took his attention away
from the beach to point out some of the exotic plants and
birds the island possessed, going into such detail that she
knew he hadn't just stopped with owning the island. He
had made it his business to know all its various aspects,
so that those areas that needed protection were given it.

After a while Zoe wandered down to the water's edge.
Removing her shoes, she paddled in the shallow waves,
kicking up spray and watching the myriad droplets turn
to prisms in the sunlight. Shaking back her hair, she
raised her face to the sun, and in doing so she missed her
footing and slipped to her knees. She breathed in the
salty tang of the sea and laughed, turning her head to
watch Ross as he walked along with eyes lowered. He
squatted to inspect a find, turning his back slightly, and
the sun glanced off the play of muscles and sinews as he

moved. Zoe couldn't tear her eyes away from him, and her hands tingled with the desire to mould his firm flesh beneath her fingers, to feel him respond to her touch. She remembered how cool and smooth his skin had felt, and how quickly it had begun to burn under her carresses.

Then all at once he moved and she found him standing completely still, watching her, his face arrested. She felt the curling wave of warmth spread through her at his expression. It was a recognition of her own emotion closely followed by the flaring answer of his own. On this level at least, they communicated perfectly.

It was a moment out of time. Unable to withstand the heat of his eyes, Zoe lowered her own, and when she looked up again a second later, Ross had moved on. She came to her feet too and continued along the curve of sand, but she was conscious now of watching eyes. What was he thinking as he looked at her? Had she given herself away? If the eyes were truly the mirror of the soul then her face must surely reflect her love for him for, try as she might, she couldn't always hide it. But then again, what you see in a mirror depends on who is doing the looking. Not looking for love, Ross might only see desire.

About half-way round the island Ross suggested they stop for a swim and a rest. Zoe agreed readily, for her skin was prickly hot and carried a sheen of perspiration. She laid out her towel, then quickly stripped to her blue bikini and ran down the sand and into the water. Ross passed her as she surfaced from her dive, a dark shape that cut through the water like an arrow. Through the crystal clarity she traced the shimmering line of his body and long powerful legs, then he was gone in the glare of sun on the rippling surface. He broke surface in a burst of rainbow spray a short distance from her and stood up in the waist-high water, legs braced apart against the swell.

As his arms rose to sweep the water from his face, Zoe dived again, her quick strokes sending her shooting through the water to dart between the arch of his legs. Then, with a quicksilver movement she twisted, grabbed hold of his calf and pulled for all she was worth. Taken completely by surprise, Ross collapsed sideways just as Zoe surfaced, gasping for air. She barely had time to gulp down a breath before a pair of strong hands manacled her ankles and pulled her feet out from under her. She went down with a yelp and an inelegant windmilling of her arms.

When she surfaced, gagging on the salt water, Ross was only a foot away, laughing at her. 'Brute! Philistine!' she accused.

'What's sauce for the goose is sauce for the gander,' he mocked before striking out away from her with strong sweeps of his arms.

They swam for a long while, until they began to tire, then waded from the water to collapse on to their towels. Zoe lay looking up at the cloudless blue sky. It was beautiful but she felt a little sad. It had been like this that last day on Crete. Then she remembered that the day had not ended there. They had gone back to the hotel and made love, not falling asleep until the sky had already begun to lighten on the horizon. They had barely made it to the airport for the booking-in time. That made her laugh.

She heard Ross sit up beside her and turned her head towards him. He looked amused but puzzled. 'What's so funny?'

She sat up too and put out a hand to smooth away the smallest of frowns from between his brows, 'Nothing. I'm just happy.'

The warmth in his emerald eyes replaced her laugh with a slow throb deep within her, and when he took her hand and placed his lips against her palm, her heart did a flip-flop in her chest.

Ross closed her fingers over his kiss and shook his head. 'Priceless!'

Zoe looked down at her folded hand, swallowing painfully to hold back a sudden surge of tears. Hastily she turned to lie on her stomach when they refused to stop. She felt his hand at her waist, soothing.

'Zoe?'

She didn't move. 'I'm all right.' Her reply was muffled. She knew he wouldn't be satisfied with that and added, 'I felt a little dizzy. I'll be fine in a minute.'

She could feel the stillness of disbelief transmitted to her through his hand and then the warmth of his touch was gone. From behind closed eyes she heard Ross sigh and get to his feet, then his footsteps crunched up towards the treeline. A few minutes later he was back.

'How about something to eat, you must be hungry.' His voice came from close to her left ear.

'I left my magic wand behind,' she mumbled into the towel.

'Did you?' he asked in amusement. 'We'll just have to manage without. What do you say to roast chicken, rolls, cheese. Um ... salad, pickles ...'

Zoe sat up in a hurry, blinking in bemusement at the picnic hamper beside her, rubbing at the traces of tears and quite forgetting he wasn't supposed to know she had been crying. 'How ...?'

Ross raised his hand, palm towards her. 'How,' he intoned with a grin.

Startled, it took her a second to realise he was playing the fool to cheer her up, which meant she hadn't deceived him at all. 'Idiot!' she laughed, loving him for the thought. Especially as it was something the old Ross would have done automatically but which she had come not to expect from the new. 'All right, how did you do it? And don't forget, this injun pretty smart woman.'

His rich laugh was music to her heart. 'George ran it round in the dinghy before breakfast,' Ross admitted as he deftly uncorked the bottle of wine he produced from a cool box. Filling two glasses, he held one out to her. 'A toast—to the most beautiful woman on the beach.'

She sipped the wine with relish, shivering as the icy liquid traced its way down her throat. 'There's hardly any competition.'

'There's no contest, so far as I'm concerned.'

Zoe looked at him doubtfully, but Ross smiled and nodded. She cleared her throat in some confusion. Compliments were something she wasn't used to from him, and it wasn't easy to accept them unquestioningly.

'I heard you played golf yesterday. Who won?' Her enquiry was light, but remembering her moments of panic, she grimaced inwardly.

'Not me,' he admitted sorrowfully.

Zoe bit her lip. 'Oh? Somehow I thought you'd be good at it.'

Ross finished his wine and laughed. 'I was playing under a large handicap.'

'Doesn't everybody, unless they're very good? My father plays and I believe he has a handicap of ten. What's yours?'

'You.' He invested that one word with a husky sensuality that reached nerves deep-buried.

'Me?'

'You. I've never hooked and sliced my way through a game like that before. Instead of concentrating on addressing the ball, all I could think of was the way you had felt in my arms.' He grinned wryly. 'I was so busy wondering what you were doing back here, half the time I was miles away. God knows what Rick and Helen thought. It was a relief to reach the nineteenth hole and drown my sorrows.'

Laughter bubbled out of her. 'And did you?'

He laughed at himself with ease. 'What do you think? Rick packed me off home with the recommendation that I should bring whoever she was with me next time, or give up golf.'

'So you promptly threw your clubs overboard, did you?' she teased.

His eyes gleamed. 'I think I'd rather take you with me.'

Zoe floundered in her responses to the message he was giving out. 'I'm here with you now,' she replied breathlessly.

'Aren't you though.' Green eyes caressed every visible inch of her and set up a delicious tingling. 'And I'm very, very glad of it. Want to know why?' His voice deepened to a husky growl.

Zoe shivered, unable to take her eyes away from his. 'Why?'

'So you can be an angel and rub some lotion on my back. I can never reach it on my own.' He waited until comprehension swept over her face, before turning on to his stomach, chuckling.

'Why, you rotten devil!' Zoe gasped indignantly.

He wasn't going to get away with that. With a determined jutt of her chin she rummaged in the hamper for the bottle and unscrewed the lid. With a feeling of unholy glee she squeezed a large cold dollop right into the middle of his back. Ross let out a yell of shock but before he could roll over, Zoe planted both hands on the lotion and began to rub it in vigorously.

Ross subsided with a groan, relaxing the muscles that

had tightened with the shock. '*Mea culpa, mea culpa,*' he moaned shakily.

She relented then, allowing a small smile to curve the corners of her mouth. Dreamily she let her thoughts wander as her hands softened to smooth the lotion over his skin. He had always been a terrible tease, but now, as then, he wasn't going to get it all his own way. He used to find her attempts at reprisal amusing, but even so there had been times, like now, when she had succeeded. She could feel his muscles flexing under her ministrations and knew he wasn't immune to the stroke of her hands. She traced the indentations of his spine down to the material of his briefs, then up again over his ribs. Only gradually did the knowledge her fingertips relayed to her brain register on her consciousness and then she looked down at his broad back. Dotted haphazardly across almost the whole surface were small, pale scars.

With a sense of sick despair she ran her hands over them, tears welling up, blocking her throat and misting her eyes as she really saw him for the first time. He must have been in agony and she hadn't been there to help him. Damn them! Damn them all!

When a tear landed on her hand Zoe knew she would be unable to carry on. Abruptly she moved away, falling face down on her towel, hiding her tears against her arms. She felt rather than heard Ross lift himself to look at her and then the warmth of his hand burned against her shoulder.

'Finished?' He tried to tuck her hair away so that he could see her, but she turned her face the other way.

'Yes.' Her voice was muffled and almost obliterated by tears.

She had no strength to stop him when he turned her over on to her back, but she kept her reddened eyes hidden behind her lashes. Ross leant over her, balancing

on his forearms. With gentle fingers he eased her hair
from where her tears had glued it to her cheeks. A deep
frown etched his forehead as he traced the droplets that
glittered against her lashes.

'Why the tears?' His voice was gruff and mystified.

Zoe's lips trembled and she raised her lids to look into
his concerned face through the rain-drenched gold of
her eyes. She moved her hands to frame his face, fingers
urgently tracing the lines of his cheekbones and the
forceful chin. 'All those scars, Ross!' Tears welled again,
making it impossible to utter another word.

Ross couldn't have looked more surprised. He wiped
her tears away with hands that were far from steady.
'You mustn't cry for me, Zoe,' he chided softly.

'Don't say that!' she cried angrily, uncaring of what
she might reveal. 'Don't ever say that! I want to cry for
you. I want to have the right to cry with you!' she
sobbed, tossed between anger and bitterly remembered
torment.

Stunned into silence by her outburst, Ross had
difficulty removing a constriction in his throat. 'Oh
God, you unman me!' He lowered his lips to kiss away
the tears.

Only then did Zoe realise what she had said, that her
words had been those of a woman in love, not of a
woman caught in a fleeting romance. He couldn't have
mistaken it, and yet he hadn't spurned her. Far from it.
A gasp of mingled joy and hope left her lips as she
became aware he was still speaking.

'We'll cry together if we must, sweet Zoe, but not for
this. Not for something that happened before I knew
you. So dry your tears, darling.'

'Oh, Ross,' she breathed on a sigh, blinking back
threatening moisture.

'That's better. You're very sweet to be concerned for

me, but there's no need. I've only just realised I don't
like seeing you cry. I much prefer the way I felt when I
saw you wading out of the sea, for all the world like the
girl in the Bond film.'

That brought a watery smile back to her face, and she
slipped her hands round his neck to curl her fingers in
his hair the way she had wanted to do. 'You lusted after
me, you mean.'

Ross grinned incorrigibly, ignoring the way she
tightened her fingers in his hair. 'I wanted you, that's
true, but I don't know if it's strictly accurate now.'

'Does that mean you've lost interest?' she wanted to
know, because his body against hers was telling her
something totally different.

That made him smile. 'Far from it.'

'Then?' she prompted, feeling a thrill of excitement
starting to spread through her veins.

He chose his next words carefully. 'I think you're a
woman whom it would be foolish of me to dismiss
lightly—the way I have been doing. I was wrong to keep
seeing you as a carbon copy of my ex-fiancée.'

It dealt Zoe a vicious blow to hear him confess he had
been going to marry another woman, but she hid it well,
waiting to hear if he would tell her more or change the
subject as he had done before. This time, though, she
didn't wait in vain.

'I suppose I ought to explain. It isn't a very nice story.'
Absently his fingers toyed with a lock of hair. He
sounded grim and his eyes were far away. 'You see, it
wasn't only the likeness between you, though God
knows that was purely superficial, it was the fact that I
let myself be taken in by such a bitch. What the hell was
there about her that I let my good judgement be
overruled by lust? For fifteen years or more I've avoided
getting trapped into any relationship, yet a woman such

as she turned out to be must have had something about her. Christ, if I could only remember!' Abruptly he halted his passionate speech to refocus on her troubled features.

At least she had caught a glimpse of the reason for his ambivalent behaviour. It was his own integrity he was doubting. But at the same time she felt a degree of confusion that she was at a loss to explain. It niggled at the back of her mind but found no answer.

'What did she do, Ross? How did she hurt you?' Perhaps the answer to that would shed some light.

His face was savage. 'The love of my life, the beautiful woman who swore undying affection, left me while I was lying in a coma in the hospital. Did she offer to stay and help bring me out of it? Oh no, she couldn't stomach the idea that I might be some kind of vegetable if I recovered. She came to the hospital just once, and when she heard the odds she left. Even my parents couldn't persuade her to stay, to wait and see. The one woman I had chosen to love and trust turned out to be a first-class bitch who wanted my money more than she wanted me.' Ross stopped as he caught sight of her distraught face. 'That shocks you, I see.'

Shocked? Zoe was horrified. If she hadn't heard it with her own ears she wouldn't have believed it. He was talking about her! The facts were wrong, but there couldn't be any mistake about who. Somewhere he had gathered together a story that just wasn't true, and the worst of it was, that knowing the true story she still couldn't confront him with it. Even if she could have spoken, she didn't have any doubt of Ross's reaction if she baldly stated that she was his fiancée. He would want to kill her. He would be worse to her, knowing who she was, than he had been when he didn't know.

My God, she thought wildly, what do I do now?

What can I do? The harsh questions were followed by an agonisingly harsh answer. There was nothing she could do.

'I told you it wasn't nice,' Ross reminded her, recalling her to the fact she was still lying in his arms on the beach, not in the middle of a bad dream.

Zoe watched him through wide, stricken eyes. 'No. It wasn't. It was the . . . the worst tale I've ever heard,' she pronounced faintly, but truthfully. 'Are you . . . are you sure it's true . . . what she did?'

'As sure as a man can be when he can't remember a goddamn thing about it,' he returned bleakly.

'Then how . . .' she began the obvious question, but Ross cut across it.

'My family told me, and they have no reason to lie.'

Oh, didn't they? She had different memories of his parents. Things became clearer to her then. So they hadn't taken her word as enough. They had made certain of her alienation by feeding their son a string of lies that she couldn't refute. They had been quite diabolically clever. With hundreds of miles between them, they had still been able to force her hand.

She had to clear her throat before she could speak, but even then it was little more than a croak. 'Didn't you try to find her for yourself, just to make sure?'

'I tried to find her with the express purpose of wringing her no doubt beautiful neck. However, with the cleverness of her kind, she disappeared. No doubt the name she gave my parents was a stage name, for there was no record of it anywhere. In the end I was glad I didn't find her, she wasn't worth going to prison for.'

At least now she had one answer. His parents had given Ross a false name because the last person they would have wanted him to find was her—and so discover the truth. There was no base they hadn't covered. And she had found out too, why Ross felt he had let himself down. He needed to know why he had fallen so heavily for the wrong woman so that he could prevent the same thing happening again. She couldn't tell him that it just wasn't true, that he had no need to fear for his integrity. To do so she would first have to tell him why he should believe her, and in so doing would convince him that he shouldn't. The trust had gone.

And what if Ross should discover her identity now? The outcome of that was too frightening to contemplate.

'Hey.' Ross gave her a little shake. 'I wasn't trying to upset you. I wanted you to understand why I'd given you such a rough time.'

'I do understand, it's just that I find it very hard to believe that any woman could be as bad as she's been painted.'

'That's because you have a kind heart. It's a dog-eat-dog world we live in, Zoe. It's a hard school, and some of us learn the hardest lessons too late, but once we do learn, we never make the same mistakes again.' He smiled then, because he realised how troubled she still was. 'My tale of woe wasn't meant to distress you. The salutary lesson was mine, so cheer up.'

Her heart was saying impossible, even as her brain forced a smile to her trembling lips. Argument was out of the question and so was the truth; prevarication was her only resort. 'I'm sorry. It's just that what you told me reawakened memories of my own.'

'Of the man who gave you the ring? You were engaged?' The concern in his voice was an irony in itself.

A wave of hatred at what was being done to her wiped the smile from her face. 'We were going to be married.'

Ross held his breath. 'What happened?'

Zoe focused on the strangely fragile features above her. 'I lost him. He was taken from me,' she whispered forlornly. Oh God, it was unbearable having to speak of him as if he wasn't just inches away. I think I'm going to go mad.

'I'm sorry.'

If anything that was worse, to hear his sorrow for someone he thought he didn't know. 'You mustn't be. I got over it.' She swallowed and carried on with determination, 'Besides, I've met you now, haven't I?' If he rejected her now, she would be lost for ever.

Ross's smile was slow and full of warmth. 'Yes, you've met me. You know, you and I could be good for each other, if we give ourselves the chance. Help us to forget old wounds.'

'I'd like that,' she confessed, 'I'd like to put the past behind us.'

For a fleeting moment a haunted look filled his eyes, then it was gone again, hidden from view so that she couldn't be sure she'd seen it at all.

'We'll seal the bargain in the time-honoured way,' he declared, then his head blotted out the sun as he bent to press a lingering kiss to her lips. Tentatively, Zoe sought to respond to the tenderness, but his lips feathered on, dropping butterfly-soft kisses on her eyes and forehead, down past the sensitive skin behind her ear, to settle finally on the pulse-beat that fluttered at the base of her neck.

Zoe tangled her fingers in his hair as his exploring lips traced their delight-invoking path. She wanted to kiss him too, but he evaded her efforts to draw his mouth back to hers. Thwarted, she pressed her lips to his shoulder and let out a little gasp as his skin burnt beneath her touch. Ross raised his head and their eyes met, the banked green fires in his turning hers to molten gold. Only then did his lips crush hers once more, driven by a compulsion neither wanted to withstand.

Passion flared instantly as their lips met, eagerly exploring each other. Teasing, biting—probing with consummate skill the moist sweetness, darting and stroking, building up a need that cried out for appeasement. Pulling away from the drugging kiss, Ross explored the taut, tender cord of her neck with lips that branded their way to where her pulse hammered in wild excitement. One large hand settled possessively on her waist, moving out and across the fluttering expanse of her stomach, drawing lazy circles with a tender pressure that set up a throb that rocked her. Heat travelled up to her breasts, swelling them against the inadequate covering of her bikini, her nipples so sensitive that each breath she took sent them to mould against his chest, surging wave after wave of aching pleasure through her body.

She caressed him in her turn, delighting in the sound of his muffled groan as her fingers trailed along his spine and up again. Then she was moaning too as strong male fingers slipped the triangles of cloth aside, and his lips left hers to close upon their new objective. A wave of feeling so intense swept the breath from her as his tongue teased the proud flesh until she cried out.

A small sob escaped her when Ross lifted his head, raising his eyes to hers. The desire for her that was revealed in his flushed face and slumbrous eyes, thrilled and unnerved her at the same time. It overwhelmed her, making her senses riot, creating a need she wanted to fulfil but was suddenly almost afraid of. Would this be all that Ross wanted, a brief but heady passion? She needed to be sure there was more, but their response to each other got in the way, misting everything in the haze of desire.

Zoe's brief moment of awareness vanished in a flood of pleasure as Ross let his hand trace a path from her breast down across the gentle swell of her stomach to close tightly about her hip and urge her yet more closely to the urgency of his body.

It was then they both became aware of the intrusive throb of an engine coming ever closer and stiffened into immobility. Ross sat up, cursing freely at the interruption. He scanned the water of the bay and saw the craft round the small headland bare moments later.

'It's—Pete, I think—in the dinghy.' He glanced round to where Zoe lay still with her eyes closed. She opened them when she felt his look. 'You stay here, I'll go see what he wants.' He gave her one darkly frustrated stare, then rose to trot down to the water's edge.

Zoe sighed deeply and adjusted her bikini. Her whole body ached with the abrupt cessation of their lovemaking. She was as tense and quivering as a bowstring, and could only guess at Ross's feelings. She sat up, folding her legs into a semi-lotus position, and studied the physical beauty of the man she loved. Upright and strong, full of gentle power and grace, he alone had the ability to draw from her the full measure of her passionate nature.

As if Ross sensed her eyes upon him, he turned from watching the dinghy to wave at her. She waved back, glad that he could not see the brooding look in her eye nor the vulnerable tremor of her lips. If he had seen, how could she have explained that her fears were because just when his feelings about her were undergoing a change, he gave her news that made it even more difficult. His parents' actions filled her with anger and disgust. No doubt they believed they had won, but they wouldn't do that while she had a breath left in her body. She wouldn't give them the satisfaction, not after what they had done to their son. What she needed now was time to think of a way out of this maze.

She watched Pete beach the dinghy and climb out to stand talking to his boss, then Ross swung about and strode purposefully back towards her.

'I'm sorry, Zoe, but we've got to go back. Mike's had a frantic phone call from my offices in Australia. All hell seems to have broken out.' He started to pack up their belongings as he spoke.

Zoe gathered up their towels and clothes, forming them in a rough bundle. 'Did he say what it was?'

'No, just sent Pete to find us. Damn, why did it have to happen today?' he muttered angrily, slamming down the lid of the hamper and securing the pegs. It took less than a minute to be ready to leave, and mere minutes to cover the distance back to the hotel in the dinghy.

Back on land, Ross turned to Zoe, taking her chin between his fingers. 'This may just be a storm in a teacup. Why don't you go and have a shower and then come up to the bungalow and wait for me. We can have dinner together. There's no reason why the rest of the day should be spoilt. I'll be as quick as I can.' He planted a swift, hard kiss on her lips that still bore witness to his earlier assault on them, then turned on his heel and quickly walked away. Within a dozen paces Zoe knew she would be gone from his mind. His business would always call him. She only hoped this time she would be with him long enough to get used to it.

CHAPTER SIX

Ross didn't make it for dinner—or supper either. Showered and changed into a turquoise blue wrapover dress in crinkled cotton, Zoe waited patiently but in vain. It gave her ample time to think but produced no answers save the obvious. She needed to build a solid relationship that would stand the revelations she had to make, and for that she needed time.

She hadn't meant to fall asleep, but the emotional upheavals of the day took their toll. The deep, comfortable cushions of the couch eased her into sleep, but the further she fell, the more her defences dropped, leaving her relaxed brain no shield when the nightmare came again.

Just like all the other times, suddenly she was plunged back into the swaying, clattering train. Trapped in a carriage that was full of people all talking and laughing, but she couldn't hear a sound save the clackety-clack of the points. She was searching desperately through the faces but the far end of the car seemed to be growing darker, fading away as the noise grew ever louder until it was a scream that echoed the frantic beating of her own heart. Something awful loomed towards her from the darkness and she opened her mouth to scream a warning but it turned into the hideous screech of metal that was cutting its way into her body, colouring everything blood-red.

Then the scarlet slash dissolved into a pair of lips that laughed and taunted as she struggled in the grip of invisible bonds. She saw him then, a shadowy figure that moved away from her and she knew she had to follow

115

him but they wouldn't let her—they wouldn't let her—
they wouldn't let her . . .

And she screamed and screamed.

She called for him in a voice that cracked with pain.
Then magically it became her own name, calling to her,
bringing her back from the edge of despair. With it came
a sense of peace so all-encompassing that tears fell from
her eyes. She turned into the arms that reached out to
enfold her—and woke up.

Zoe stared up into Ross's pale, strained face, his green
eyes dark with concern. She knew instantly what had
happened, she always did. You never forget a nightmare
the way you do a dream. She still felt sick with the
horror, her shuddering body drenched with
perspiration.

'Are you all right?' He sounded shaken.

'It was a nightmare,' she stammered with a shudder,
burrowing closer to his broad chest. The steady beat of
his heart was immensely comforting. He was warm and
strong, and in his arms the horror began to recede.

Ross gave a sort of strangled laugh. 'You're telling
me? You scared the hell out of me. I heard you
screaming as I came up the lawn.'

Zoe was shocked. 'I didn't know I was doing that, I'm
sorry I scared you.' She tipped her head up as she spoke,
and as she did so her cheek found the open neck of his
shirt. With kaleidoscopic brilliance the world tilted and
changed. She was assailed by the scent of his body and
the tingling brush of the hair on his chest. The muscles
in her stomach twisted and a rush of heat spread
outwards to every pore. The nightmare was forgotten as
all her senses were suddenly concentrated on this flaring
of intense physical awareness.

'You were calling out my name, I thought you were
being murdered, at the very least.' Ross didn't seem

aware that the reason she was now shivering in his arms had nothing to do with the trauma he had interrupted.

Zoe watched his lips form the words, hearing them as if from the end of a long tunnel. Her body was in a state of flux, undergoing a molecular change at the close proximity of his. She could see the growth of beard on his jaw and her imagination could feel the sensual rasp of it against her skin. Her lips parted as she watched his mouth, and her flesh prickled.

'It was very—unpleasant,' she murmured, but she couldn't remember it clearly at all. Everything was fading in the face of this new feeling. She dragged her gaze from the mesmerising movement of his lips, seeking his eyes, watching him through heavy lids. His eyes were a deep, dark mysterious sea-green. She wanted to fall into their depths and discover all the secrets they shielded, to make them blaze with the fires of passion until they saw nothing but her.

The pink tip of her tongue appeared to moisten her lips, and as she did so, she felt his stifled gasp and found Ross was sitting absolutely still watching her. Their eyes locked, and against her cheek she could feel his heart start up a rapid rhythm. Everything inside her went liquid as she saw the colour rise in his cheeks and the febrile glitter of his eyes.

The heat of his body burned her through her clothes, the air around them thick with tension as he lifted one hand to trail a finger over the quivering lips, probing the tender inner skin until she caught it between her teeth and bit down gently. With a muttered oath Ross jerked his hand away, and her groan was swamped by his as he pulled her mouth up to his. The plundering of his lips and the sensual glide of his tongue seeking hers with hungry force impelled her head backwards and she arched herself against him, her arm going up about his neck as she pressed closer to the hard maleness of him.

His hand slid its way inside her dress, finding the swollen globe of her breast, thumb teasing the thrusting nipple into a proud peak until she gasped against his mouth, drowning in a pool of desire. Then his lips were removed from hers and their parted moistness blazed a fiery trail down the column of her neck until they closed over the throbbing mound his fingers still enclosed.

Zoe's lashes fluttered and closed as his flickering tongue and nipping teeth wrought havoc on her senses. Ross's voice was muttering thickly against her breast, but his words meant nothing to her. This was what she had been made for. Everything culminated at this point where she and Ross lost their individual selves and became one.

She could feel the pleasure he was experiencing at her response, the surprise in himself that his own response had been so strong and immediate. When he raised his head to look at her, studying the hectic flush on her cheeks and the bruised lips, he shook his head as if to clear it.

'My God!' The words came thickly from his throat. 'I was supposed to be comforting you, not ravishing you!'

Zoe gave a faint throaty laugh, 'You haven't . . . yet.'

His eyes were riveted to hers, but his hands were running forays over her back beneath her dress. 'You're in shock. You don't know what you're doing.'

'Yes, I do,' she insisted huskily, running her fingers into his hair, seeking out the strong bones beneath. 'I'm seducing you.'

His hand came up and framed her face. 'Not if I seduce you first,' he declared indistinctly.

'Can't we . . .' she broke off on a gasp as his fingers found the sensitive skin behind her ear, 'can't we seduce each other?'

His lips came down perilously close to hers. 'Thank God for compromise!' he groaned with a half-laugh before his lips met hers in a long drugging kiss that sent them spinning way out of control.

The fact that they hadn't intended this to happen was unimportant; there was no way either of them could stop now. Need overcame all other factors. This was necessary as breathing ... the very stuff of life.

Both were short of breath when they next drew apart. His eyes asked a question and hers replied, then he was coming to his feet with her locked tightly in his arms. Zoe cast her arms about his neck as he carried her to his bedroom, burying her lips against his throat, feeling the tell-tale beat of his pulse increase at her caress. His head dipped, urging her to meet the demand of his mouth as he let her slide to her feet by his bed. Unsteady fingers found buttons and zips, moving eagerly until their clothes were gone and they met each other half-way. Parted lips locked in a heated exchange while quivering limbs moulded flesh to flesh.

The bed sagged under their combined weight as, legs unable to support them, they sank on to it, locked in a feverish embrace that made them both gasp and moan. Piercing waves of white heat sent them shuddering along a path of beautiful destruction. Ross's thickly muttered words of praise and encouragement invited her abandoned caresses. He groaned and trembled under her touch, relinquishing command to her. The heady delight at the power she wielded over him made her bold. Her hand skimmed his hot, sweat-slicked body until he could take no more and pulled her beneath him to assault her with long tender caresses that sought out the secret pleasure-centres of her body and made her writhe against him.

'I want all of you,' he muttered, rising above her to press heated kisses against her cheeks and throat.

Her hands brought his mouth to hers. 'Take all of me,' she offered with abandoned generosity.

She welcomed his possession, arching her body against him, matching his slow, sure strokes that built up the spiralling coil of tension. His mouth covered hers as she moaned out her pleasure, only tearing away when the fierce contractions caught them in a rip-tide, making them both cry out in exaltation and consciousness gave way to oblivion.

A long time later Zoe stirred beneath the weight of Ross's spent body and he sighed and raised himself to his elbows over her.

'Are you prone to nightmares?' he asked, smoothing the damp tendrils of hair away from her face with unaccustomed tenderness.

Her eyes widened in surprise. 'Not very often. Why?'

Ross half laughed and tweaked her chin. 'I was just wondering how often I can expect to be seduced.'

She couldn't help laughing. There was no feeling of shame or embarrassment, for they had met as equals, even if Ross had no way of knowing that he was also the recipient of her love.

'If you imagine I'm going to suffer a nightmare just so that you can enjoy yourself, you've got another think coming.'

Ross grinned, easing on to his side, making himself comfortable on one elbow. 'So, tell me, what was it all about?'

Zoe took the hand that rested on her waist and threaded her fingers through his. 'It was about the accident I was involved in.'

'That was where you lost the man you were going to marry?' He latched on to the obvious connection quicker than she expected.

'Yes.'

'It can't have been very long ago, then.'

'No, not very,' she sighed.

Ross studied her carefully, his eyes thoughtful. 'Do

you want to tell me what happened?' he offered.

Zoe shook her head, more moved than she could say by the gentle consideration in his voice. 'It would serve no useful purpose.' Save to remind him of his own hurts and his anger at her supposed treachery. She didn't want that. She wanted nothing to mar the beauty of what they had just shared.

'No,' he agreed, 'it only opens wounds that are better left alone.'

'What you can't forgive, you must forget,' she ventured hesitantly, watching anxiously for signs of anger to appear on the relaxed lines of his face.

None appeared. Instead he nodded reluctantly. 'I know it, but it's easier said than done. Our pasts aren't so very dissimilar. It must have hurt you when I accused you the way I did. I can only plead ignorance. Normally I wait before jumping down anyone's throat. I apologise for that.'

'Will that make me the exception or the rule?' she charged drily.

'The exception,' he returned, as she had expected. So he hadn't changed his attitude to women of her profession, only herself. Not that she was complaining, it would be a novelty not to anticipate the rough side of his tongue. 'After my less than gracious behaviour, I was surprised when you responded to me the way you did. When you give, you give wholeheartedly, don't you?' he went on, making her blush for the first time.

'It's better to give than to receive,' she stated, not quite meeting his eyes, because as a statement it was not quite accurate.

She watched his face register disbelief. 'Well, it solved another mystery. You weren't a virgin,' he said outrageously, which had the effect of sending her gaze to lock with his in shock.

She took a deep steadying breath, 'Disappointed?' she asked.

Ross threw back his head and laughed. 'Oh, no, darling. Not under the circumstances.' His emerald gaze wandered leisurely from her head to her toes and up again. 'This man you loved . . . he was your first lover?'

It was her turn to laugh. 'How many do you think I've had? Until you, he was my only lover,' she confessed.

That came as a big surprise, and she felt his shock in the tensing of the hand that lay in hers. 'You're serious?'

'Of course. I've no reason to claim lovers I haven't had.'

Ross looked stunned. 'Hell! Are you telling me . . . why did you let me make love to you?' As she watched, the perplexity turned to suspicion. She knew what he was thinking.'

'I wasn't looking for a substitute for him,' she hastened to say with complete honesty. There could never be a replacement for Ross. 'I'm an emancipated woman. I believe in the freedom of choice. I chose you.'

His brows rose at that. 'Why?'

'Because I wanted to. Because I needed you, and it was right. I have no regrets. Do you?'

One hand framed her face. 'No, but this changes nothing. You understand that?' His eyes assessed her reaction.

Oh yes, she understood very well. He might not believe her to be the fickle woman of his imagination, but he was not about to become involved with any woman. If she expected to win him over, he was telling her quite clearly she was wasting her time. She wasn't surprised, even if it had the power to hurt. She kept her expression clear of all emotion.

'You made yourself very clear. I mustn't fall in love with you. Is it all right if I like you?' she asked openly.

Ross frowned as if she had said something he didn't

understand, which in a way she had. She wasn't giving up anything. She wouldn't fall in love with him because she already had. She wouldn't find herself loving him because she had done that too. Want it or not, if he agreed to let her like him, he would get the other two in spades.

Eventually the frown disappeared. 'Liking is allowed. You're a rather likeable little thing yourself.'

Damned with faint praise! 'I have my good points. One of them is that I expect nothing of you. You're free to do entirely as you like.'

His eyes gleamed with a roguish light. 'That's a very sweeping offer. By it you mean I can do anything I want?'

Her heart started fluttering in her chest. 'Absolutely.'

His body curved over hers, one leg pressing her into the mattress. 'In that case, I want to make love to you again.'

Zoe began to chuckle, sliding her arms up and round his neck. 'That's your choice, I'm not going to expect it of you,' she teased, rolling her hips, knowing by his response that he wasn't free to refuse.

Ross knew it too. 'You are the most aggravating . . . surprising . . . exciting little baggage I've ever met,' he said, punctuating his words with kisses.

'And you want me,' she breathed unsteadily.

'And I want you,' he agreed thickly.

Her arms pulled him down to her, 'Now that you've got me where I want you, stop talking and make love to me,' she ordered huskily, and, making a sound between a laugh and a groan, Ross did precisely that.

Whether he liked it or not, things were different after that. They couldn't be otherwise. They had become lovers, and although that meant very little change for Ross, it was an emotional committment for Zoe. They were as close as he would allow, which was totally physical. His thoughts and feelings he still kept very much to himself. It was his everyday attitude that changed.

He seemed to stop actively looking for similarities between her and his ex-fiancée, and stopped saying cutting and hurtful things. She didn't know if it was the things she had told him which brought about this change or not. What she did know was that he relaxed and became a charming companion. Not quite, but almost, the man she had known on Crete.

He didn't realise she loved him, of course. She kept that well hidden. He didn't know that in the way she laughed and joked with him, and in the boundless giving of herself when they made love, she was, in fact, loving him deeply. She knew she could never batter down the defensive walls he had put up, so she tried to undermine them instead.

Ross had had to fly to Australia after that day on the beach when Pete had been sent to find them—bush fires had destroyed one of his properties—and he had come back after a week's hard work, looking more drawn than ever. It was in this low state that she finally managed to get him to slow down, but only, she guessed, because he had already chosen to. When she wasn't working, they spent the long sunlit hours playing tennis, or swimming, or simply relaxing on the beach. And, of course, they made love.

Through it all Zoe gave him her love unstintingly. Sometimes she thought she saw signs that he was coming to love her a little in his growing thoughtfulness, but in the next instant he would be shutting her out again, and she realised it was just wishful thinking. So she made a determined effort not to be downhearted. Already she had gained more than she ever expected, and she experienced an almost superstitious feeling that to rush too much would lose what she had.

She was marking time, hoping that proximity, rather

than absence, would make the heart grow fonder. Yet as the days went by, all she saw was the growth of friendship and no more. It was brought home to her one afternoon after they had trekked into the heart of the island and come to rest by a spring up in the hills.

They were lying side by side soaking up the sun. A short while ago they had made love, and now they were at peace, letting the soft rustle of leaves and tinkle of water envelop them. Zoe watched a brilliantly hued bird dart out of the shadows into the sunlight, searching for food to feed the family chirping in the tree it had just left. Unconsciously her hand probed the gentle curve of her stomach.

'Don't you want children, Ross?' she asked idly. He had before, but now . . .

After a pause he said on a strange note, 'Are you trying to tell me something?'

'No.' He knew she took precautions well enough. 'I meant, don't you want an heir? Someone to carry on your name and all your businesses.'

'Having been brought up with that tradition, I wouldn't wish it on any child of mine. But as I have no intention of marrying, the prospect doesn't arise,' he replied brusquely. 'Besides,' he added, 'children should have parents who love and respect each other.'

'Don't you think you could find love?' Zoe asked, holding her breath until it was painful.

He laughed, deeply amused. 'I'm not looking for it. Why the sudden interest?'

She shrugged, plucking at the grass under her fingers. 'No reason. I was just wondering, that's all.'

Ross rolled over on to his elbows and studied her. 'Tell me, if you had been pregnant, would you have expected me to marry you?'

Her eyes shot to his anxiously, and seeing his closed expression, her lids fluttered down to hide her thoughts.

'Well, I wouldn't be averse to marrying you.'

His hand came out to turn her face towards him. 'Look at me,' he commanded, watching as she reluctantly obeyed him. 'Is that what this is all about? Are you hoping that I'll marry you?'

She lost a little colour. 'No,' she lied, 'I thought we were having a hypothetical conversation.'

He stared at her a long while before he seemed satisfied. 'Good. We have the perfect relationship. I'd hate to have to give it up simply because you've got some crazy notions in your head.'

Zoe swallowed a lump the size of a tennis ball. 'I hope to get maried one day.'

He smiled and rolled on to his back again. 'If you send me an invitation, I'll even come and dance at your wedding.'

She should really have left it there, but she couldn't. 'Why don't you want me to fall in love with you? I mean, you wouldn't have to return the feeling,' she demanded, stiffening in anticipation of his answer.

Ross sighed disgustedly. 'There would be no percentage in it, but I couldn't stop you.'

Zoe winced. Well, she had had to ask, and she couldn't complain if she didn't like the answer. Only there was something she had to know. 'Don't you have any feeling for me at all?'

'Damn!' Ross swore and rolled over again, this time looming right over her. 'Such as?' he asked impatiently.

Zoe looked away. 'Oh, forget I asked!'

'Little fool!' he muttered, forcing her chin round. 'Zoe, I like you. I enjoy your company and I thoroughly enjoy taking you to bed. Isn't that enough?'

If she said no, that would be the end of everything, and if she said yes, she would be lying. To salve her pride she took the middle road. 'It's enough to be going on with.'

Ross didn't miss the subtle distinction and his lips twisted wryly. 'Then we'll close the subject. And now, my little wood nymph, having kept me from sleep, the least you can do is apologise.'

She allowed him to distract her. 'How?' she teased.

His head obliterated the sun. 'You have three guesses.'

Zoe pulled his head down, and, grinning, whispered in his ear. With a growl Ross buried his lips against her throat.

'Right first time,' he acknowledged, accepting her apology even if it took a very long time to be said.

So they went on. Zoe hid her bruised feelings beneath a cheerful exterior. If this was all Ross wanted, then she wouldn't let him see that she wanted more. She would simply have to work harder to convince him that he did want all that he was determined to deny, and that she could give it to him.

CHAPTER SEVEN

WISHING hadn't made it so.

Silvered waves lapped at Zoe's feet as she stood gazing pensively out over the moonlit water. It was well past midnight, and she had come to seek peace for her troubled thoughts.

Ross knew her now as well as he ever had, perhaps better, but still he showed no signs of needing more from her. They had a—passionate friendship—a status quo of emotions that guarded his inner self. So well did it work that Zoe didn't know if it hid something that was there, or something that was not.

Yet he watched her, all the time. He showed interest in everything she said and did, as if she were a complicated puzzle he was determined to unravel. Apart from her identity as his fiancée, she had hidden nothing from him, so she had no idea what he was searching for. The only assumption she could make was that he was still expecting her to walk away. He didn't trust any woman to stay faithful. Even with all her giving he didn't believe she was different.

For weeks now he had put work into the back seat, spending more and more of his time with her. But while Zoe welcomed it, it also served to point out the lack of real involvement. If only he could have shown her one sign that he cared, that his solicitude went deeper than that of a generous man to his lover. If only he would let her in. She didn't even know what he would do when he left Mariposa, or even when that time would be. It was a silence that weighed increasingly heavily on her heart.

That was why she had come down here, to stand silently watching the flow of the tide. Tonight there had been an extra dimension to their lovemaking, almost desperation on her part, and they had come together fiercely, reaching heights of passion never scaled before, but later, a cloud of despair had settled about her. She had left Ross after he had fallen asleep to wander down to the beach, hoping the wash of the surf would make her unhappy thoughts go away, but they stayed with her.

The truth was as unremitting as the tide. Ross did not love her. It was that simple. He liked her, desired her, showed no signs of growing tired of her, but that was all. So, what happened next? The answer came surprisingly easily. When it came down to it, the important question was not did he love her, but did she love him enough to stay with him knowing he didn't return her feelings. The answer to that was yes.

Zoe gave a sigh that echoed loudly on the still night air. Unconsciously the waves set up a rhythm that summoned a memory. She could find a song for every mood, but 'Come Rain or Come Shine' seemed particularly apt to her tonight. Without effort, the words themselves poured out.

When the last line faded away on the night air, Zoe knew the peace she sought had found her. She watched the moonlight ride in to the beach on the backs of the waves. Slowly and silently it went about weaving its magic, and that must be her way with Ross. Given time, her love could wear away his defences. She turned then, to retrace her footsteps up to the bungalow, and froze. Ross stood no more than a few feet away from her. How long had he been there? Had he heard her song, and did he understand what it meant? She went cold inside.

'What is it, Zoe? I woke and you were gone,' he asked softly, making no move to come closer.

She came out of her surprise with a start. 'I couldn't sleep,' she murmured inadequately, feeling strangely unable to close the small gap between them. Sometimes an inch could be wider than an ocean.

'I know. It's happened a lot lately. That's why I came looking for you.' His voice was non-committal, but she recognised an undertone of concern.

She hadn't been aware he knew she left his bed so often, and she had no idea what he made of it. She wished she could see his face more clearly. He sounded— distant, a stranger again.

'I'm sorry. You didn't need to do that,' she apologised without knowing why. Unless it was for bringing him from his bed to these surroundings in the middle of the night.

'I almost wish I hadn't. You were a million miles away from me. You must miss him very much.'

Zoe couldn't pretend not to understand him, and it seemed a cruel kind of joke to say, 'Not nearly so much now that I've found you.'

She was unprepared for his abrasive laughter. 'You know, I really think you expect me to believe that.'

Zoe gasped at the violence behind his words. 'But it's the truth.' She never thought she would have to defend that statement. Her mind was whirling. The next thing she knew, Ross had crossed the sand that separated them, one hand fastening on her chin to stop her from avoiding his eyes.

'The damn man's never out of your mind!' he accused, his controlled anger sounding all the more intense for being held in check.

She couldn't believe this was really happening, and what was worse, it was hopeless to attempt an explanation. She was left with voicing an inadequate, 'Oh, no, darling.'

He looked down at her, questioning her words. Abruptly he let her go, jabbing his hands in the pockets of his robe and taking a couple of impatient steps away from her. 'Do you think I can't see when you're not with me, Zoe? Damn it, I want your whole attention, not just part of it. If this man's in the past, leave him there. I'm with you now.' He turned his head to stare at her.

She closed the distance quickly, cupping a hand to his rugged jawline. 'That's where I want you too, Ross. You're a vital part of my life now. If I think of him . . .' Her throat closed. She felt as if she was going crazy. She swallowed madly and managed to shift the blockage enough to finish. 'If I think of him at all, it's fondly.'

'Yet it's enough to bring you out here in the middle of the night,' he insisted.

Zoe closed her eyes for a second. 'Ross, you aren't telling me you're jealous?' She made herself sound disbelieving, but inside she was willing him to say yes and prove she meant something to him.

He looked angry. 'No, I'm not. It just appears to me you can't let the past go.'

Disappointment added an edge to her words. 'You're the one saying that. I know where the past lies.'

'Forgive me if I find that hard to believe,' he came back at her sarcastically. 'Your being here proves it.'

'You're making an issue out of something you say means nothing to you. Forgive me if *I* don't believe *you*.'

'This is ridiculous!' he exclaimed exasperatedly.

Angry herself, Zoe balled her hands into fists. 'You are so right. To be jealous you have to care, and you don't, do you?'

'I said I wouldn't,' he bit out, taking hold of her shoulders. 'So why are you upsetting yourself like this?'

Her laugh held a note of hysteria. 'Did it never occur to you that I might wonder about what happens to me when you leave? You won't be staying for ever. Even I can see you're much better than when you came.'

Ross swore. 'You go with me, of course.'

While her heart did a leap, her main reaction was anger. 'There's no "of course" about it. So far as I knew, I was just your holiday fling.'

He swore again. 'You're more than that and you damn well know it.'

She faced up to him furiously. 'How can I? I'm not a mind-reader.'

That made him stop and stare at her. 'Hell!' Anger drained away, and he pulled her into his arms. 'I'm sorry. I assumed you would understand.'

'So, I continue being your mistress?'

Ross went rigid. 'Don't use that term, it's degrading,' he commanded shortly.

'Then what would you have me use, Ross?' she demanded, yet feeling a curling warmth invading her at his tone. She sensed him about to say something, but then he stopped, and it was a minute before he spoke again.

'When I think of one I'll let you know,' he concluded abruptly. 'Are you coming back now?'

Zoe nodded. She hadn't intended forcing the issue, but she was glad now that she had spoken, for Ross hadn't quite closed the door on her future; in fact, he had left it interestingly ajar. Maybe it was a moot point, his dislike of the term mistress, but he could have easily found a few other words to say the same thing and not offend his sensibilities. Only he hadn't, and it was that hesitation which rekindled the spark of hope.

Zoe stirred to an insistent buzzing and groaned, rolling on to her stomach and trying to bury her head beneath her pillow. The sound persisted and resolved itself into the hiss of the shower, and she turned to sit up against the headboard, tucking the silk sheet under her arms. The sound of singing floated above the water and Zoe winced. Strange how a man with so rich a voice couldn't hold a tune. His singing stopped, and Zoe, however much she loved him, was glad.

Ross wandered back with a towel slung low about his hips. He was whistling as he pulled on shorts and a cotton vest, and that was off key too.

'Are you going to lie there all day?' he asked, and ran a proprietorial eye along the line of her body beneath the silk sheet. 'You'll be late if you don't shift your delectable little body.'

Zoe blinked and stretched. 'Late? It's Saturday, a day of rest.'

'Come on, or you'll spoil my surprise.'

'What surprise? Are we going somewhere?'

Ross only laughed. 'Now, if I told you, it wouldn't be a surprise, would it?'

'At least tell me if I dress up or dress down,' Zoe requested, slipping from the bed and making for the bathroom.

'Anything casual,' he called after her departing figure, 'and your bikini. Do you still have the white one? I have fantasies about you wearing that.'

Zoe appeared in the doorway and threw a soggy sponge at him which missed and put a permanent stain on the wall. 'No, I do not have that damn bikini. I threw it out. So you'll just have to fantasise about something else,' she replied sweetly.

Ross neatly fielded the sponge in the slips and lobbed it back. 'That's OK, sweetheart, I also dream about you with nothing on. Look, I've got to go. When you're ready meet me down at the jetty.' He was gone before she could follow up that clue.

Half an hour later, dressed in baggy white shorts and soft cotton top over her bikini, and a few other items she had thought of tossed into a bottomless bag, she wandered down to the jetty and found Ross on board a streamlined yacht that lay docked there. Pete was tinkering with the engine under Ross's watchful eye, and Mike stood watching them.

Pete saw her first as she stood surveying the scene. 'Hi, gorgeous.'

Zoe waved, eyeing the sleek lines of the boat with growing excitement. 'Are we going in this?' she called.

Ross looked up. 'If Pete remembers how to put it all back together again. He had his nose in the engine before I got here.'

She appreciated now why he had left in a hurry. She jumped nimbly aboard, and Ross was there to catch her as the deck heaved beneath her feet. Gold eyes laughed into green. Pete, re-emerging from the depths, eyed them with a grin.

'Ain't love grand.' He winked at her before jumping ashore and disppearing into his workshop.

'Sure is,' Ross agreed as he set her on her feet again.

It was Mike who witnessed Zoe's stunned face. 'Are you OK?' he asked quietly.

'I'm fine,' she insisted, but her smile was wobbly. That must have been the throwaway line of all throwaway lines, but had she heard him aright? Had he actually said that about love? Oh God, she hoped so. It would be too cruel if he had not.

Ross turned back to them. 'Everything OK?'

This time Zoe's smile was stronger. 'Yes, I just had to get my sea legs.'

Ross's smile was a warm caress on her skin. 'Good.' He turned to his friend. 'Do you think you can cast off for me?'

'Sure,' Mike agreed. He slipped the moorings and lifted a hand in salute. 'Have a nice day.'

Zoe waved back then turned her eyes seawards. Ross didn't speak to her until he had successfully navigated the boat out into the open sea. Only then, with the clear expanse of blue-green water before them, did he turn to where she was standing beside him.

'Are you going to tell me where we're going?' Zoe asked politely, though with the prospect of a day's sailing their ultimate destination was unimportant.

Ross slipped his hand round her waist and drew her close beside him, 'We're going island-hopping. When we get further we'll stop the engine and hoist the sails.'

Smiling, she put her arm around his shoulder, massaging the firm muscles under her fingers. 'Mm, sounds marvellous.'

Ross caught her hand, pulling it up to his mouth and nipping at the sensitive flesh. 'I thought that would appeal to you. It also has the advantage of putting us beyond the reach of the telephone. Why don't you stow your gear below and get into your bikini. There's room to sunbathe on the deck up forward.'

Zoe did as he suggested, and they set course for the day. The boat had been designed for easy handling by one sailor, but they shared the pleasure of getting the best out of her between them. There were hundreds of islands in the group and they navigated round quite a few of them, taking the opportunity to stop and soak up the sun and have a drink before they sailed on again. The temperature soared at mid-day, and Ross dropped anchor in the lee of a small island and took them ashore in an inflatable dinghy. They picnicked on fruit and wine and delicious fresh bread, before succumbing to the somnolent rays of the sun. By late afternoon they were ready to go on, and Zoe was thankful for the cooling breeze created by their forward motion as she lay in the shade of an awning. It wasn't long before she drifted off to sleep again.

When next she opened her eyes the boat was no longer moving, save the gentle motion which told her they were at anchor again. She yawned, stretched and sat up, searching for Ross, but she was alone. She rose gracefully to her feet and made her way astern. The first thing that met her eyes was a beautifully laid-out table, then she saw Ross. He lay stretched out along the banquette at the stern, eyes closed, hands tucked behind his head, completely at ease.

She had thought he was asleep, but he opened an eye as she approached. Smiling, he held out a hand and drew her down on to the seat beside him. She smiled too, lowering her head to press a kiss into his shoulder. Resting over him, her hands idly stroked the flat planes of his chest.

'Hi.' His voice was as rich and relaxed as the rest of him.

'Hello.' She ate him up with her eyes. She loved it when he was like this, too comfortable to move, just happy to be with her. 'You spoilt my surprise. I was going to wake you with a kiss.'

'Be my guest.' His eyes crinkled as he smiled at her.

She bent and touched her mouth to his. His lips were warm from the sun, and she teased them with her tongue. Ross's hand came up to frame the back of her head as he returned the caress.

Zoe eased away a few inches. 'You taste of peaches.'

'Um-hm. I snuck one while you were asleep,' he admitted with an unrepentant grin.

'Just like a man to feed himself and leave the rest of us to starve,' she accused.

Ross sat up with her in his arms. 'I debated waking

you, only you looked too comfortable. But seeing you're awake, I'd better feed you. I left the food in the galley. Why don't you take a seat while I fetch it,' he suggested, standing up and ruffling her hair as he passed.

Ross produced a veritable feast of succulent meats and spicy salads. Nothing had been spared, and there was champagne to wash it down. Zoe laughed, shaking her head, and helped herself to a little of each.

'No expense spared?' she teased, when she sat back, unable to eat another crumb.

'I like to see you happy. You don't smile enough.'

She peeped at him through her lashes. 'Are you going to make it your self-appointed task that I do?'

Ross sat back, smiling. 'It seems a worth-while occupation.'

'You mean you'd give up your work for it?' she teased again.

'Probably,' Ross agreed, much to her surprise.

Zoe's jaw dropped. 'You can't mean it?'

'I rarely say things I don't mean, Zoe,' he said, resting his chin on his hand and regarding her steadily.

She sat up a little straighter, desperately uncertain of how she was supposed to interpret his words. 'Your work means a lot to you. To give it up would mean . . .' she faltered in the middle of the minefield. It was too incredible.

'That I love you,' he finished for her.

Zoe shook her head slowly. He sounded sincere, but she couldn't believe him, however much she wanted to. Last night he had said nothing. What made today different? Oh no, he was testing her, that had to be it.

So she laughed. 'You'll get over it.'

For a moment Ross went still, then he laughed too. 'You're probably right.'

Well, that certainly told her she was right, but it hurt

like the devil. Heartsick, she rose abruptly to her feet and
crossed to stand at the rails. The moon was rising and
there were the first faint glimmerings of stars overhead,
a romantic setting which had nearly caused her to make
a fool of herself and believe his odd humour. After a
while she sensed Ross behind her.

'It's getting late. Mike will start to worry,' she said.

His hands came to rest lightly on her bare shoulders.
She sighed and hunched into them. It didn't do to dwell
on his earlier remark.

'No, he won't. I radioed while you were sleeping and
told him not to expect us until morning.' Ross brushed
his hands over the soft down on her arms. His warm
breath on her neck heralded the brush of his lips on her
nape. 'You don't have any objections?'

She gave a smile he couldn't possibly see. 'None at all.'

'Fancy a swim? The water should still be warm,' he
suggested, running a series of kisses down her neck and
along her shoulder, making her shiver.

'Yes, please.'

She felt Ross's groan vibrating down her spine. 'You
have a way of saying that which makes the blood rush to
my head,' he moaned into her ear.

Zoe gave a wicked little laugh. 'A swim will cool your
ardour.'

His voice dropped about two octaves. 'If you believe
that, you'll believe anything. But you're the kind of
woman who needs proof.'

Zoe guessed his intentions even before he attempted
to catch her about the waist, and she snaked away from
him, going over the side in a sleek dive, cutting the water
with scarcely a splash. With quick strokes she put as
much distance between herself and the boat as possible
before treading water and looking back over her
shoulder. There was no sign of Ross anywhere, so she

turned on to her back and swam slowly towards the shore.

She didn't realise Ross had joined her until his nimble fingers disposed of the ties of her bikini, and by then it was too late. She spluttered upright with a cry of indignation.

'I suppose you think that's funny,' she cried in outrage.

Ross didn't answer her, but jack-knifed to come up behind her and pull her backwards until her body was lying on his and he towed her to shallower water. Shallower, that was, for him. When he came upright, his feet were touching the seabed but hers were not, and the gentle tide swept her in to his body. It was then she realised that he was naked too.

She gasped as her breasts met the wall of his chest, but he forestalled her attempt to move away by fastening his hands on her waist and holding her firmly to him. Zoe was forced to hold herself away with her hands on his shoulders. Though it allowed her to see him clearly, it also forced her to lock her legs with his to maintain her balance, and that contact took her breath away again.

Zoe found it almost impossible to think of anything save the silken glide of flesh on flesh as the tide ebbed and flowed around them. And her brain stopped functioning altogether when he lifted her until he could nuzzle one perfect peak with his lips. She felt her nipple harden as it was drawn into his mouth and the pleasure was almost pain.

Ross relinquished his torture with a groan. 'That, my darling, was to show you just how wrong you were. There isn't a power on earth that could keep me away from you,' he declared, his husky voice vibrant with passsion. 'Let's go back. Suddenly swimming is the last thing I want to be doing.'

Zoe had just enough strength left to get her to the boat, but she needed Ross's help to clamber aboard. She was shivering too, by then, but not from the cold. Ross grabbed a towel, wrapping it around his back and drawing her in to his warm body, enclosing them in the soft folds of material. Zoe let her hands rest on the hair-roughened skin of his chest and reached for him with her lips.

For long minutes they were locked in a passionate embrace, then Ross jerked his mouth away from hers, sucking breath into his lungs with a pained gasp. 'God, how I want you. You can't know how much!'

'Yes I do. I feel the same way,' she breathed raggedly. 'I don't care that you feel nothing for me, I'll take what you can give for as long as there is,' she confessed, losing control of her tongue.

The towel disappeared and a pair of strong hands framed her head, turning her face up. His eyes blazed at her with an emotion she had given up all hope for. Incredibly, heart-stoppingly, it was there now. 'You're wrong, oh, so wrong, Zoe. You should have believed what I said before. I love you.'

Silent tears forced their way from her eyes. 'But you don't believe in love,' she insisted against all the evidence.

'Didn't. Now ... well now I feel something for you that, if it isn't love, I don't know what else it is. Nothing else comes close to describe it.' Gently Ross tried to instil belief into her with his eyes and hands.

It was hard, after all this time, to drop her defences. Too much suffering had gone before. 'How long?'

'I think the presence of you has been working on me for a long time, but I didn't admit how I felt to myself until last night. It hit me like a ton of bricks. You asked me if I was jealous, if I cared, and I realised that I was, I did. Then I had to decide what I was going to do about it. I didn't know how you felt about me, but I had the idea that maybe you did love me a little. That gave me the incentive to carry on. I know I've done nothing to make you believe me. When I said what I did about love, I genuinely believed it was true. But you made me see that what it came down to was that I was scared of making the same mistake again. How could I, who had shown such lack of judgement, be sure that what I felt wasn't exactly how I had been before? Then I knew I was truly being a fool because, although I can't remember her, there is just no way you fit the description, so my own feelings must be different too. If you were prepared to take the chance again, why not me too? You can't know how I felt when you gave me the chance I wanted and then laughed when I told you.'

'But I thought you were testing me. I didn't know . . .'

Ross closed her lips with his hand. 'I know. I don't blame you. I was pretty unpleasant when we met.'

Zoe's heart was thumping out a rapid beat, and her eyes were still awash with tears that were a mixture of pleasure and sadness. 'Are you really sure?'

He pulled her closer. 'Yes, I'm sure. All along you've been telling me you were different, and you are. You're unique. Beautifully, wonderfully unique. I'd be a fool to cling on to old prejudices and lose your love. That is if you do love me.' There was a ragged edge to his voice as he formed the words.

Zoe was crying in earnest. 'Oh, Ross, I love you so much. I wanted to tell you but I was afraid to, because you said you didn't want it.' Her voice was little more than a wobbly whisper.

'I was protesting too much,' he breathed shakily against her lips, revealing just how much her confession meant to him.

Impatient now with words, their kiss was a passionate seeking and confirmation. They clung together, lashed by fiery tongues of love and desire. Searching again and again for the deepest responses from the other, exulting when they found no bounds. The doors behind which their love had been hidden were now open, and a whole new world of feeling was born.

Exultantly Ross swept her up in to his strong arms and carried her down to his cabin, stretching the lissom length of her upon the soft sheets, joining her with a look on his face that was almost of pain. They came together and both were trembling. Every touch of lips and hands was electric, causing a response that was like nothing they had shared before. Ross's hands moulded her to him, stoking fires, pushing them out of control. He traced the graceful flow of her back, down over her hips to her thighs as if her skin were made of gossamer, searching out all the secret pleasure-centres until she was shivering and moaning in his arms.

He raised his head and looked at her, smiling when she turned glazed, passion-filled eyes to his. Then his fair hair was all she could see as he lowered his head to her breasts. His lips paid homage to her bounty, teasing and stroking, stirring the globes into hard-pointed peaks with flickering strokes of his tongue. Though he smiled again when he lifted his head once more, Zoe could see the tension in his eyes.

'Touch me.' He groaned out the plea that Zoe responded to with a fierce pride. He abandoned himself to her caresses, muscles trembling under her hands, not ashamed to moan in answer to the pleasure she gave him.

He was truly hers, as she was his. Nothing was held back. Zoe was swamped with sensations, floating away dizzily on pleasure so profound it left her almost sobbing. They moved together with growing urgency, their heated bodies striving to break the bonds of the physical, their limbs clinging damply. It was too intense to delay that final, most beautiful joining. When at last his body took hers, she cried out, words of love spilling from her lips. Her abandonment was total, but still Ross had enough control to delay the moment with slow movements, even as the sharp contractions of her body urged him on. It couldn't last for ever, and with a groan he at last yielded to their mutual craving and drove them both on a gasping tide of excitement towards a spiralling, white-hot climax. They scaled the heights to freefall back to earth, locked together for all time.

After endless moments the world righted itself again. The tiny cabin echoed to their laboured breathing, but in time that too ceased and they were at peace. With a sigh Ross eased himself on to his back and carried her with him so that she was cradled on his chest.

'Now do you see how much I love you, Zoe?' he declared softly. 'How could I give that up? I'd be poorer than the lowest beggar if I even contemplated it. I never expected to feel this way. I only know it couldn't have been this way before, or I would have remembered. A love like ours couldn't be forgotten. The best thing that ever happened to me was when she walked away. It allowed you into my life and you aren't going to leave it,' Ross vowed with such a depth of sincerity that Zoe had to work hard to keep from crying.

Suddenly she was terribly afraid of what would happen if he should ever discover that she and his fiancée were the same woman. She hadn't thought about it because the possibility of Ross coming to love her had grown so remote, but now, after what they had just shared, it came to her just how much she could lose. She would have to tell him eventually, for the danger of his finding out from any other source was too great. Ross had told her he didn't see much of his parents, but the time would come when he was bound to want to introduce her to them. She thanked God they were a whole continent away, travelling in Europe. They were the dark storm clouds on her horizon, but the winds were in her favour, holding them off.

'I love you so much,' she declared huskily. 'Don't ever leave me, I couldn't bear it.'

He thought she was thinking of her dead lover. 'Darling, I've no intention of going anywhere without you. I'd sooner cut off my right arm. You have to believe me. This is for ever.'

She did believe him, she really did. Only ... 'Your parents?'

Ross laughed. 'You can leave them to me. They know better than to interfere in my life. They have a strong tendency to manipulate people, but they gave up on me a long time ago when they realised it would never work. Believe me, you have nothing to worry about.'

Zoe sighed. It wasn't easy to trust when she knew things he didn't but she had no other choice. Resolutely she pushed their spectre back in the dark corner where it belonged. Ross would tell her when he intended to visit his family. Time then for her to worry. The present was for Ross and herself, their plans and promises.

For the first time in many long months, Zoe fell asleep content.

CHAPTER EIGHT

THEY slipped back into the calm waters of Mariposa's harbour early next morning. Ross steered the craft gently towards the landing stage and Zoe jumped ashore with the line and deftly made it secure. She did the same with the stern-line Ross tossed her, then waited for him to join her on the jetty. He held his arms out to her with a fond smile, and she slipped into them with a satisfied sigh.

'Still love me?' He whispered the question between kisses.

'Quite desperately,' Zoe admitted, surrendering to the practised torture of his embrace.

Ross wasn't immune to her brand of enchantment. In danger of drowning, he pulled away. 'You do realise we're in full view of the hotel?'

'If I close my eyes they'll go away,' she grinned.

He laughed and dipped his head to kiss her again, 'Well, my beautiful ostrich, I think . . .'

Whatever his thoughts, he never got to voice them, for a feminine voice hailed him and their heads turned to see who it was. They both recognised the couple waiting at the end of the jetty, but whereas Ross smiled and lifted a hand in greeting, the joy was swept from Zoe's face and she felt icy fingers of dread closing about her heart.

Oh, dear God, it couldn't be! But it was, her horrified eyes told her. She would never forget their faces as long as she lived, as they would not have forgotten her. Cole and Deirdre Lyneham! She felt sick, and perspiration broke out on her forehead. How many times had the thought of this meeting made her cry out in her sleep? Her heart beat out a death knell. They were just forty or fifty steps away. A short walk to the end of everything.

There could be only one outcome to the meeting that was only minutes away. They would tell Ross who she was. They would build on the story they had told him before—and Ross would believe them. The lead weight in her stomach warned her of that. She had been hoping to postpone any confrontation until he trusted her more, until she could tell him herself, safe in the knowledge he would believe her.

That was all in the past now. She had to play with the hand she had been dealt, but she was so scared. It was like going back in time to that day after the crash when they had rejected her. It was going to take all her nerve to walk up to them and believe she could win.

Ross taking her hand distracted her painful thoughts. 'My parents,' he explained, nodding in their direction, unaware of Zoe's hysterical need to laugh at the unnecessary introduction. 'They can be a bit overpowering, but whatever you do, don't let them intimidate you. Just smile and be yourself. Their bark is worse than their bite, I assure you.' When Ross slipped his arm about her waist, he couldn't miss the trembling that had taken her over. 'Hey, what's wrong?'

She turned desperate eyes on him, clamping down on panic. 'I must be nervous,' she forced out between dry lips.

His smile was sympathetic, and his hand tightened reassuringly on her waist. 'You have nothing to worry about.'

She licked her lips. 'You do love me, don't you?' she asked urgently. 'Nothing will change that, will it?'

He was surprised by her vehemence. 'You're overreacting, darling. You couldn't have got enough sleep last night.'

She ignored the sally. 'If . . . if things don't turn out as you think, what will you do, Ross?'

He grinned, shaking his head at her. 'The only one you have to please is me. If my parents don't like you, that's their loss. Now will you stop all this worrying.'

She tried to look as if she wasn't, but her heart was thumping madly. Frantically she tried to think. She knew what she should do. She should tell him the truth before they got to him and distorted it all, but to do herself justice she needed time and privacy, and there just wasn't any. Already Ross was urging her along to where his parents waited. They halted before the couple and Zoe watched with a sinking heart as Ross shook hands with his father and kissed his mother's proffered cheek.

At first the couple only gave her a cursory glance, concentrating on their son, explaining how they had decided on the spur of the moment to find out how he was progressing. Inevitably all three turned back to her, and it was then, with their attention fully on her, that she saw the recognition remove what friendliness there had been from their smiles. Her mouth went dry and she could't utter a word.

Something in her stance must have struck Ross as odd for he gave her a puzzled smile as he slipped his hand back to her waist. 'Zoe, let me introduce you to my parents,' he began, only to be forcefully interrupted.

His mother's hand went to her throat. 'My God, Ross! What's she doing here?'

Zoe blanched. Ross's hand gripped her waist tightly and she looked up quickly. His face showed a look compounded of surprise and offence. 'I beg your pardon?'

Deirdre looked aghast, as well she might, considering she didn't know what, if anything, Zoe had told her son. 'You fool! It's her, that flightly piece who abandoned you.'

Ross laughed abrasively. 'Zoe? Have you gone mad?' he demanded.

His mother bristled. 'No, but you must have. After all she did, how can you even look at her? I suppose she thinks she can crawl back into your bed now you're well again.'

Zoe let out a gasp, anger welling up inside her. She had to defend herself because she knew fatalistically that denial was useless. 'That's a wicked lie.'

Out of the corner of her eye she saw a movement Cole Lyneham made and misinterpreted it, sure he was about to strike her as he had had no compunction about doing before. She flinched away.

'Guilty conscience, my dear?' he queried mockingly.

'Not at all,' she came back quickly, feeling her heart beating anxiously. 'I thought you were about to hit me. You showed no scruples when I only had one good arm to defend myself.'

Ross turned incredulous eyes on her. Her heart twisted in anguish at their bleak question.

'None of what they said is true!' she burst out furiously, but Ross had already picked up on her distress and was able to interpret it with this new information, and it was damning.

'Mother, be absolutely sure before you throw out accusations. Are you telling me Zoe was my fiancée?'

Deidre knew then that Zoe had told Ross nothing, and she flashed the younger woman a triumphant glare. 'That's precisely what I'm saying. She came to the hospital, found you were in a coma, and we never saw her again. Even so, I would know her anywhere.'

'How can you lie like that?' Zoe challenged, a dreadful feeling of impotence filling her.

'You can't contradict me.' The fact was flung back in her face, and Zoe winced. Everything the other woman had said was true, only the interpretation of it made the difference. 'Look at her, Ross. Surely you can see the guilt all over her.'

Ross looked and saw, for Zoe's face showed all her anxiety at his parent's arrival and the 'truth' they had revealed. There was sufficient fact among all the fabrications to make her despair. She couldn't even begin an explanation with his parents watching. They had played a master-stroke months ago and time had been on their side. She had to get him alone.

Despairing, Zoe clutched at Ross's arm. 'Ross, we have to talk.'

'You're damn right we do,' he ground out coldly, and moved away so that her hand fell, leaving her with humiliated colour staining her white cheeks. He turned to his parents. 'You'll understand I have to deal with this now. We'll meet again later.'

Deidre wasn't happy with the idea but she could hardly argue. 'Of course we understand, darling. Perhaps you ought not to be too hard on her. Sending her packing will be just as effective.'

'Save your pity for those who need it, Mother,' Ross suggested, and Zoe echoed the sentiment for different reasons. Deirdre's hypocrisy made her feel ill.

In silence Ross led the way to his bungalow. With tight-lipped control he pushed her into the lounge ahead of him and leant against the door jamb, watching silently as she crossed the room to stand near the cocktail cabinet.

'Seeking Dutch courage, darling?' he taunted.

She shook her head, she hadn't been conscious of

where her feet were taking her, only that she felt the need to put some distance between them even as she wanted desperately to close the gap that had opened.

'I don't need it,' she denied, wishing she didn't feel so cold inside. A sense of fatalism was growing within her.

'Does anything throw you a curve?' he enquired bitterly, in a voice as smooth and cold as steel.

She flinched away from his scorn, but took her courage in both hands. 'Don't do this, Ross. Listen to me, please. Losing you last time almost killed me, this time ...' she faltered and swallowed hard. 'Don't condemn me until you've heard me out.'

'So you've given up denying who you are.'

'There wouldn't be any point, would there?'

'How long did you think you could carry out this deception? My God, how you must have laughed when you realised I didn't remember you. No doubt you were hoping it would stay that way until you got a ring on your finger,' he derided icily.

Zoe paled. 'I already have your ring.'

'So you do. I'm surprised you didn't sell it.'

Her eyes smarted with unshed tears. 'I've been telling you how much you mean to me all these weeks, Ross. You know I couldn't sell the only link I had with you.'

Ross studied her in silence. Nothing she said appeared to have reached him. He had closed her out.

She was finally forced into defensive speech. 'Stop looking at me like that.'

Ross's smile was grim. 'Like what?'

'As if I'm a stranger.'

A muscle jerked in his cheek. 'You must forgive me, but the woman I was introduced to just now is not the same one as last night,' he bit out brutally, pushing himself upright, easing a tightness in his neck and shoulders.

His words drew her a few paces towards him. 'That's not true. I'm still the same person. I still love you, very much,' she exclaimed passionately.

'Cut out the dramatics. You might be a good actress, but it only works if your audience doesn't know the plot. So, I'm the fiancé you lost so tragically in an accident, am I? What was the point of the sob story, Zoe? Or can I guess. If I had a sudden return of memory, at least you would have covered all the bases. How unfortunate for you that my parents should turn up this way and reveal you for the gold-digging bitch you are,' he condemned bitterly. Repulsion etched harsh lines on his face as he watched her.

Zoe flinched, her colour draining away. 'It wasn't as you think. They lied to you, Ross,' she said, desperation taking hold.

His laugh was harshly unbelieving. 'For what reason?'

One hand raked her hair. 'I'm not good enough for you. I sing for my living. When I came to the hospital they wouldn't let me see you. They wouldn't listen to me. They had me bundled away and they made sure I stayed away.' Her eyes pleaded with him to believe her.

Ross crossed the room, seizing her retreating figure, shaking her hard. 'Why don't you speak the truth for once in your deceitful little life? If there's one thing my parents know better than to do, it's interfere in my private life.' He released her abruptly, as if her touch revolted him.

Distress and anger mixed, making her shake. 'Don't you care? They showed no compunction. They enjoyed destroying me, watching me break down.'

'What a vivid imagination you have,' he jeered down at her.

It was too much. Her hand shot out and dealt him a

resounding slap on his cheek. Violence flared in his eyes, and before she could move, Ross clamped her head between hard hands and crushed her lips with his. He relieved his anger with bruising force, grinding her lips against her teeth.

Then he thrust her away with a harsh expletive. Zoe raised a trembling hand to her lips, probing their soreness with her tongue.

Tears set her golden eyes awash. 'I'm telling you the truth.'

'You wouldn't know the truth if it jumped up and hit you,' he snarled. 'Everything you've told me has been a pack of lies from start to finish. All the hesitations and evasion that I believed, fool that I was, came from a great loss, were nothing more than a smokescreen. God! No wonder you made it so easy for me to have you. You were begging for it. How far did I come down the list of the men you've jumped into bed with for their money? A long way judging from the tricks you've picked up.'

'Don't, Ross,' she begged, contaminated by the insults he flung at her. He was going to leave her with nothing.

'Don't what?' he questioned silkily. 'Don't tell the truth? I have no aversion to it as you have, my dear Zoe.'

'I've always told you the truth,' she cried desperately, wincing as his fingers bit into her upper arms, knowing they would leave bruises on her tender skin.

'Tell that to the Marines!' he scoffed.

'Listen to me. Oh, please, listen to me. If you can't take my word for it, ask John.' She made a last ditch effort to reach him.

'What the hell has he to do with this?' he demanded roughly.

Zoe swallowed painfully, gasping as the grip on her arms tightened. 'He was at the hospital, he saw what happened.'

For just a moment relief flickered over his face, but it was quickly gone. 'Sorry, darling, but it won't wash. I remember how uptight you got when I mentioned John to you. Now I know why. You got to him too, didn't you?'

Zoe stared at him blankly, pain visible in every rigid inch of her, 'You can't mean that.'

'Oh, but I do. We both know your appetite for sex. You could no more do without it than the rest of us can do without air. You saw a way of getting back into my life and you followed your plans ruthlessly. Using John would satisfy more than one need. You'd do almost anything to get me back, wouldn't you?' He shook her violently. 'Wouldn't you?'

'Yes!' Zoe screamed at him, driven beyond bearing by the foul things he implied. 'Yes, I'd do anthing, because I love you. But I haven't done any of the things you said. I've only ever gone to bed with one man and that's you, Ross. When you touch me . . .' a sob broke her voice. 'If you asked me, I'd never make love from this moment on to prove how much I love you, because sex without your love is meaningless to me.'

His lip curled. 'There's no need for such a sacrifice,' he mocked. 'You and I are yesterday's news. When your contract here is over, your services will no longer be required by any of the Lyneham chain.' Ross turned away, crossing the room. 'There are plenty of wealthy men who would be pleased to avail themselves of your charms—for a price. But not me. Never again me.'

Zoe closed her eyes, her throat working madly to hold back tears, but they escaped anyway. Lifting her lids, she made out his wavery outline standing by the window. She watched as he ran a weary hand around his neck and knew she couldn't leave it like this. With a sigh her feet took her to stand behind him.

'Ross, I've never done a mercenary thing where you're concerned. I couldn't, because I love you.' She took a deep breath and put a tentative hand on his arm, but Ross shrugged it off impatiently. Ready tears flooded her eyes again, and she raised a hasty hand to dash them away. 'I fell in love with you the very first time I saw you, and I've loved you ever since.' A small sob broke from her and she quickly stifled it.

Ross spun round, eyeing her bleakly. 'How very loyal of you,' he snapped, so cuttingly that she winced.

'Last night . . .' her voice dried up but she licked her lips and tried again. 'Last night you said you loved me. Today you said nothing would change that,' she reminded him.

Ross merely laughed unpleasantly. 'I was wrong, wasn't I? You can kiss undying love goodbye. I feel nothing. In fact, I'd like to see nothing too. So why don't you leave and do us both a favour.'

'Leave the island?' Misery and confusion laid her open to his attack.

The laugh she was beginning to hate came again. 'Hardly. You have a contract to honour. If you know the meaning of the word.' He turned his back on her to pour himself a drink.

She watched him in silence, biting her lips at her inability to help herself. 'Are you going to get drunk?' she finally asked, when he drained the glass at a go.

Ross swore. 'Are you still here?' he demanded belligerently.

A wave of despair filled her as she witnessed him drawing further away from her. What was she standing here for anyway? Hoping for a sudden change of heart? He had made it more than clear what he thought of her now. He didn't even want to look at her.

She paused in the doorway, holding grimly on to the

frame for support. She looked back but she couldn't see him through a veil of tears. 'I've lost you, haven't I? I've really lost you this time. You're more lost to me than if you were dead.' She saw his wavering figure stiffen at her words, but she was driven to carry on. 'I know you hate me, but I truly do love you, Ross. I want you to know that if anything should happen in the future . . . if you ever remember me, I'll be waiting for you. I'll always be there.' She wanted to say much more but she just couldn't. What control she had left was hanging by a thread, and if she didn't get out she would break down in front of him. She didn't think she could face that.

As she walked out of the room she could hear him laugh, a hollow sound with no humour in it, and her heart ached for what might have been. They were two lost souls on the way to a hell of their own devising.

CHAPTER NINE

ZOE closed the door of her chalet behind her as if that insubstantial barrier would be enough to hold back the pain, but it was something else entirely that stopped her complete collapse. As her distraught gaze surveyed the spartan contents of the room, her eye was caught by a carelessly swinging foot. Her head shot up and she stiffened when she encountered the determined figure of Deirdre Lyneham sitting comfortably in her armchair.

The older woman surveyed Zoe's distress and her lips thinned. 'You don't look well. You ought to sit down.'

Zoe called on every ounce of strength she possessed. 'Please don't pretend you care. What are you doing here?' she demanded brusquely, in no way prepared for this.

'You may not believe me, but I wish you no personal harm. I have plans for my son and they do not involve you.' Deirdre sat up a little straighter, 'You've brought this on yourself. You should have heeded my warnings. You cannot hope to win. Look at you! You're an emotional mess. Ross wouldn't listen, would he? He never will. I know my son.'

This calm stating of the obvious hit Zoe like a blow. She crossed her arms over her chest protectively. 'I can make him believe me,' she insisted.

Deirdre's perfectly manicured nails tapped rapidly on the arm of the chair. 'You won't do yourself any good. Why don't you give up and go home.'

'And leave the field open to you? You'd like that, wouldn't you? All along I've played things your way, but no more. I've nothing to lose now.' Zoe turned away, biting down hard on her lip. 'I don't know how you could do this to your son. It was inhuman.'

'It was necessary.' Deirdre's reply was unmoved, her reasoning unshakable.

'If Ross should learn the truth . . .' Zoe began, moved to horror at the cold-blooded statement.

Deirdre stood up, implacably assured. 'He never will from me, and you he'll never believe.'

Zoe faced up to her, balling her hands into fists. 'I'm not giving up.'

The older woman stared at her, as if unable to accept an attitude that could only lead to more pain. 'Do yourself a kindness, go home.'

'Ross means everything to me.' She was aghast to hear a sob in her voice. The emotional strain of facing this cold woman was destroying her control. 'If you loved your husband as much as I do Ross, then you'd know how impossible it is for me ever to give up.'

Deirdre sighed. 'So be it. I had hoped to make you see sense, but you're too stubborn. Remember this, I never make hollow threats. I admire your courage, but you're still a stupid little fool. There's no way I will ever let you win.'

'I'll never understand you,' Zoe gasped.

The other woman laughed, 'You'll never be required to.' She looked at Zoe's unhappy face. 'If you've got some liquor, I suggest you give yourself a stiff drink,' she advised. 'Goodbye, Miss Winthrop, I trust we never have to meet again.'

So do I, Zoe told her retreating back, shaking so much with the effort not to break down, that she had to collapse into her chair. She hugged her arms around her, hurting so badly that breathing was painful. She felt so cold inside. Iced up, like a deep freeze. Ross could thaw her with a look or a touch, but he wouldn't do either because he despised her.

Time was reflected in the shifting shadows on the floor, yet Zoe was unaware of it. Hours could have passed or mere minutes for all she knew. Gradually the shaking was replaced by a numbness. She was totally drained, and her head was throbbing dully. She couldn't say she hadn't been warned, but she wished to God it hadn't happened the way it had. Much calmer now, she knew she needed to do some serious thinking.

Ross was reacting blindly at the moment, but he would calm down too, eventually, and when he did, she would still have a chance if she could persuade John to speak to him. Whatever Ross had said about not believing him, she knew that ultimately he would, because the doctor had the professional ability to relay facts without emotionalism. It was impossible not to believe him. So the most important thing was to contact John immediately.

Hope, which had seemed as dead as her heart, was reborn. She refused to believe that it could be too late.

She left her chair and went to wash the signs of tears from her face. One look in the mirror over the sink left her appalled. Her eyes were puffy and bloodshot and there was scarcely a trace of colour in her cheeks or lips. She couldn't possibly go about looking like a zombie however much she felt like one. She changed into a clean top and applied make-up carefully to hide the worst of the ravages before heading for the main complex.

She found Mike in his office practising his putting stroke by aiming golf balls at a random placement of styrofoam cups. He glanced up when Zoe tapped on the door.

'Hi, come in. What can I do you for? Or have you come solely to grant me the pleasure of your company?'

When Mike saw her hesitate in the doorway, he gave her an encouraging smile. 'The coast is clear.'

With dismay Zoe registered the significance of that.
'You saw?'

Mike looked apologetic. 'I was on my way to meet
you, but they beat me to it. It was impossible not to
hear.'

Zoe stepped inside and closed the door behind her,
aware that he was studying her closely and that he would
be unlikely to miss the signs of upset.

'I suppose you must be wondering what that scene
was all about,' Zoe began diffidently, for surely Mike
would be angry at her presence on Mariposa under false
pretences. 'I owe you an explanation.'

'Shouldn't you be saying this to Ross?' he queried,
raising a sardonic eyebrow in a gesture that reminded
her more of Ross.

She took a couple of steps forward, grimacing. 'I tried
to, but there are complications. Actually, I came here to
ask if I could use your phone. I'd like to place a long-
distance call to London.'

She couldn't blame Mike looking intrigued, but he
said nothing. He went to his desk and stood his putter in
the waste basket. 'Certainly you can. You might have to
wait though.'

Zoe gave another little grimace. 'I've become a past
master at that. Oh, and could you deduct the cost from
my salary.'

Mike gave her a reproving look. 'Zoe, be a good girl
and shut up. Now, who's the call to?'

Zoe laughed a little and her face didn't crack as she
had feared it might from the tightness of her facial
muscles. 'It's to Doctor John Vernon. I have two
numbers, he should be at one of them.' She handed over
a card.

He looked at it, then at her, trying to work out the
significance of this disclosure, yet once again he said
nothing. He placed the call and handed over the

receiver, smiling. 'Somebody up there likes you. There's no delay. I'll make myself scarce and you can have my chair.'

Zoe caught his arm with her free hand. 'No, stay!' She realised at once that that sounded a bit desperate and licked her lips. Her control wasn't all it might be yet. 'Please stay, Mike. This isn't private. I've rather lost my taste for secrets and half-truths.'

Mike subsided somewhat uncomfortably, but he didn't question her request. Zoe smiled nervously and waited for the familiar voice to come on the line. When it did, tears threatened to choke her again, and she kept her gaze riveted firmly on the ceiling to hold them back.

'Hello, John, it's Zoe.'

'Zoe my dear, how delightful to hear from you.' The friendly voice was almost her undoing. 'Do I take it you have good news for me? Shall I pop a bottle of champagne?'

Zoe swallowed against a large lump in her throat and a tightening in her chest. 'It will only go flat if you do.'

A short silence echoed down the line.

'What happened?' His understanding was immediate. 'His parents arrived.'

'And created a scene, no doubt. Damn their inconsiderate hides.' Which exclamation was rather mild for the good doctor.

Whether he intended it or not, it made Zoe laugh. 'Yes, they did. They called me a lot of things. A tart and a gold-digger for starters. You heard them, you know the sort of things they said before.'

'And?'

Zoe lifted her free hand and pressed it against her eyes. 'And Ross believed them!' she whispered, her voice breaking. 'We underestimated them. They fed him a story months ago—that I had left him because he might suffer brain-damage from the coma. All I had been after was his money.'

'Good God! I'm afraid you're right, my dear, we did underestimate them, badly.' Alerted by her tone, he kept his voice devoid of sympathy. She was a hair's breadth away from breaking down.

'I did tell him to talk to you, John, but he said . . . he said . . .' Lord! How could she tell him just what he had said?

John's phlegmatic voice saved her embarrassment. 'I can imagine what he said, Zoe. And of course, not being able to remember you, his parents' version carried most weight. If I had had any idea of what they were going to do, curse them . . .! But that's water under the bridge. As I see it, I must talk to him myself. This situation cannot be allowed to continue.'

Zoe sagged with relief. 'I was hoping you'd say that.'

'No time like the present, my dear. Is he reachable?'

She turned to Mike. 'Where is Ross?'

He consulted his watch. 'By now lunching with his parents.'

Zoe passed that on, adding, 'You'd better try later. You won't give up?' she prompted and he sighed.

'If necessary I'll send in the big guns and fly out. Now stop worrying, and don't panic if it takes a few days. I can't promise the result, but he will learn the truth.'

There was little more to say, and John was a busy man, so minutes later she was replacing the receiver, feeling almost light-headed with relief. A glance at Mike showed him regarding her thoughtfully.

'Good news, huh?'

'The best,' she admitted, smiling faintly.

A shadow crossed his face but was quickly gone. 'Lucky Ross.'

'He doesn't think he is at the moment,' she amended. 'Did Ross ever tell you about his fiancée?'

An eyebrow quirked. 'Not nearly as much as you just did. Let's say, the bare bones came out as the liquor went in.'

'Did you believe him?'

Mike shrugged. 'He was pretty cut up about it, and I had no reason to argue. However, if you are she, then I have to doubt because no way, in my book, are you a gold-digger. But I'm not the one you have to convince. You don't need me to tell you you've got one hell of a job on your hands.' He pulled a face and grinned. 'You'll discover I'm not predisposed to believe Cesare and Lucrezia, and I could see for myself the change you made in Ross. Under normal circumstances, Ross wouldn't accept blindly either, but nothing about this is normal. The loss of memory has made him vulnerable. Your "defection" showed he was susceptible. Both emotions are synonymous with weakness in his book. I don't envy you the task. If it's any comfort, I'll help if I can. Why don't you tell me everything, right from the beginning.'

It meant a lot for someone so close to Ross actually to ask to hear her side of the story, and she would always be grateful to Mike for that. She took a deep breath before losing herself in the emotional whirlpool of her relationship with Ross and his family. She thought she had managed fairly well, but Mike could see the changing expressions on her face which told him, far more than mere words, how badly she had been hurt.

She faltered only once, when she had to tell of her first meeting with Cole and Deirdre Lyneham, but the rest was related in a matter-of-fact voice.

'And so I applied for the nightclub spot because I knew Ross would have to come here eventually,' Zoe finished, looking directly at him.

Mike was shaking his head. 'You seem to have placed a great deal on luck. What if you hadn't been chosen for the job?' His smile was kindly, but he was wondering if he would ever love anyone enough to go to the lengths Zoe had.

Zoe shrugged. 'I don't know. I'd have thought of something else, I suppose. I only knew I wasn't giving up. I would have come as a maid, if that was all I could get.'

'With the intention of getting Ross to fall in love with you.' Mike repeated the phrase she herself had used.

'And he did,' she added, rather unnecessarily. Mike, like the rest of the staff, had long been aware of the fact, for they hadn't troubled to hide their affair.

There was one thing she still had to know. 'Why did they do it? Don't they want Ross to be happy?'

'Ah!' Mike rubbed his nose. 'That's easy. Of course they want him to be happy, but they, Deirdre especially, would like some say as to who he is happy with. They are snobs of the first water. Ross can play with whomever he likes, but he's supposed to marry into the Four Hundred. You, sweet innocent, are the only woman Ross has ever proposed to, and not only are you not well connected, you also sing. I imagine Lucrezia nearly had a fit.'

Zoe burst out laughing at his expression. Clearly Mike didn't stand in awe. 'You managed to get by their stringent examination.'

He gave an unholy grin. 'Not only has Ross never wanted to marry a mere man, but, much as they dislike me, I am a lower-echelon member of the society they set so much store by. They think I should be running my own show, but I'm here because I like to be.'

'Good for you!'

Mike laughed briefly, then sobered up. 'Ross needs someone like you, who loves him, warts and all. He's not an easy man to get along with. He has drive and ambition, and he doesn't suffer fools. But there is another side to him, and you bring it out. He'd be a harder man if he lost you. You may not fancy bearding the lion, but you've got to keep working away at him.'

Zoe frowned. 'Go after him again now, you mean.'

'That's my advice. If you were the woman he thinks you are, you'd cut your losses. There are other fish. Sheer bloody-minded persistence might just show him you mean what you say.'

Zoe chewed her lips, the proposition held little appeal. But she was a fighter, not a quitter. Mike's explanation renewed her determination. 'I'll do it,' she stated defiantly.

'Great!' he grinned. 'Ross has always admired spunk.' He stopped and thought for a bit. 'Ross won't be free yet. You'd better come with me and I'll stand you some lunch. You can't go into the fray on an empty stomach.'

He was good for her morale. Just the boost she needed at the right moment. Going to Ross might not work, but she would give it a damn good try.

The opportunity to confront Ross never arose. When she presented herself at the bungalow with a fast-beating heart, it was to discover the building empty. She told herself he had to come back some time and sat down to wait. If he returned with his parents, then she would challenge them openly about their deceit, but she wasn't going to leave the field open to them again.

Zoe was acutely aware of the passage of time. The minutes were as long as hours and the hours turned into days before the sound of footsteps outside alerted her to someone's presence, one who wasn't Ross by the lightness of the tread. She looked up to find Marian framed in the doorway.

Her friend hovered uncertainly and waved a hand in a vague gesture. 'Hi, can I come in?'

'Please do,' Zoe invited, 'Ross isn't here to throw us out.'

If anything, Marian looked even more ill at ease. 'Yes, well, that's what I wanted to see you about actually.'

A premonition began to grow, and a sense of inevitability settled upon Zoe's shoulders. 'Your middle name wouldn't be Cassandra, by any chance?' Strange how knowing what was coming could make you extremely calm, Zoe thought wryly. 'Sit down, Marian, and tell me what's worrying you.'

Marian took a seat beside her and studied Zoe carefully. Satisfied by what she saw, she didn't beat about the bush. 'Ross has gone.'

Zoe lay back against the cushions and gave a dry laugh. How ironic. She had been waiting patiently for a man who wasn't ever coming back, when only the other week she had panicked about a man who hadn't gone at all. She stood abruptly and went to stand at the window, staring out without really seeing. She had never hated anyone as much as she did his parents in that moment. Deirdre's boast had been correct. It had been no hollow threat. She had been out-manoeuvred with ease.

'They worked very quickly,' she stated flatly.

'Who did?'

'His parents.' There was no way she could keep the bitterness from her voice.

Marian was quick to pick it up. 'Anti, are they?'

Her laugh was hollow. 'They invented the word!'

'But Ross is a big boy now. Perhaps he's just taking his parents to catch a plane and then he'll hot foot it back here.'

Still with her back to the room, Zoe rubbed her hands along her arms. 'No.'

'You can't be sure, Zoe,' Marian disagreed.

Turning to face her friend, Zoe's face was full of certainty. 'I can. Ross won't come back here.' For the second time that day Zoe repeated her story.

Marian heard her out in grim silence, then for a

blistering few seconds she made Zoe's ears burn as she
related just exactly what she would like to do to the
senior Lynehams. Zoe, who had seldom felt further
from laughter, found herself chuckling.

'Have you noticed how life is like a giant game of
snakes and ladders? Only here the snakes multiply and
when you want a ladder, somebody's just borrowed it,'
Marian added drolly.

'Don't I know it!' Zoe surveyed the room, the scene of
her worst defeat, and ran a distracted hand over her
brow, assailed by a deep wave of loneliness. She saw
Marian watching her and dropped her hand. 'Well, we
can't stay here. Thank you for coming to tell me. It
couldn't have been easy.'

Marian pulled a long face. 'Pete and I saw him go, so
we tossed to see who would tell you. I lost.'

Zoe recognised Marian was making a valiant effort to
cheer her up, and while they sipped coffee in her chalet,
she made a passable effort at cheerfulness. Later, when
Marian had gone she gave up. She felt totally enervated
and appearing cheerful had used up her remaining store
of energy.

She wandered down to the beach, finding a quiet spot
to sit and think. She would go after him, of course. She
hadn't come this far, and at such a cost, to give up, but
the number of places Ross could have chosen to go to was
so great that she could spend months trying to track him
down. She came very close then to giving up completely,
daunted by the prospect before her, but the thought of
what this meant to Ross soon reawakened her fighting
spirit. If she gave up she would be condemning him to a
future without love, and that was insupportable. Yet
what could she do? She still had her contract to work
out, and until then she wouldn't be able to leave the
island long enough to be of any use. The months of
inactivity for her would be months in which Deirdre

could add to her particular brand of poison.

In frustration she got up and walked the sands, racking her brain for a way out, her depression deepening as an answer seemed to get further and further away from her. Ross would stay out of her way. He had the means at his disposal to keep her away from any Lyneham property and in the same way to keep track of where she was at any time. Supposing he cared enough to go to those lengths. That made her stand still. If he knew she couldn't get away, he might have gone no further than New York, the centre of his operations. Wasn't that more likely? He would consider her no threat now he knew who she was. He wouldn't expect her to follow him there. The possibility of a solution made her legs so weak she sank to the ground.

Then she was struck by another blow. In all this she had been relying on John being able to talk some sense into Ross, but Ross was no longer here to hear it. Depression hit her, tearing away her paper-thin composure. She had been banking on John. He was the ace up her sleeve, but now he couldn't do her any good. Everything was going wrong, and she just didn't know how to put it right again.

She put her head down to the sand and wept. It was a long time before she raised herself upright. Finally she had had to accept it. They had won.

The memory of that day became the spectre at the feast for Zoe in the days that followed. The life went out of her. Her health began to suffer as a result. She couldn't eat. Food only choked her, and sleep was a mockery. She tossed and turned the night hours away, searching for a way to reach Ross, but always there was the memory of his disgust to defeat her.

She took to haunting Mike, hoping for news, but there never was any. He did his best, his compassion clearly visible on his face, but one day that turned to a look of horror when he caught her as the room spun round, and discovered for himself her frail, trembling body. Deeply shocked, he took her severely to task, sitting over her while she forced down some soup.

'You'll be no good to Ross or anyone if you carry on like this, Zoe,' he admonished, caught between vexation and worry.

'I'm sorry,' she muttered into her dish.

'Why don't you do something? This state of affairs can't go on!'

Zoe's stomach turned over and she pushed the food away. 'What do you suggest? I can't think of anything. All I know is that everything I've tried they've foiled. How can John speak to him when even we don't know where he is? Without John there's no chance Ross will listen to me.'

Mike halted the anxious pacing he had taken up. From outside his office window came the sound of the helicopter. 'That will be the mail,' he explained unnecessarily. Then he clapped a hand to his head. 'Lord, what an idiot. A letter could reach Ross in a matter of hours. Wherever he is, the company will forward his mail to him. That's what you must do, Zoe. Go back to your chalet and write the whole damn lot down.'

For one fantastic moment the weight lifted from her shoulders, but then it settled again. 'Why should he read it? He'll tear it up.'

'No, he won't. You know he's scrupulously fair as a rule. He was thinking with his heart, not his head, when he left. He'll read the letter even if he doesn't really want to, because that's his way. Go for it, Zoe. You've nothing to lose.'

It sounded simple, but she made many abortive attempts before she had the letter the way she wanted it. When she handed it to Mike for posting, he informed her he had to go to New York, and it would take less time if he took the letter with him. He hugged her when he saw the worried look on her face.

'Chin up! If he's there I'll force it into his hands, and hold him down while he reads it, if I have to.'

Zoe laughed as he meant her to, but she hoped it was just exaggeration, because she was already worrying enough. However, Mike seemed confident.

For a while her appetite actually returned, and she found herself eating out of sheer nervousness while she waited. Mike was gone for three days, and when he came back he handed her a shock she wasn't expecting. Before he left he had been cheerfully supportive, but now he was strangely non-committal. Yes, he had given Ross her letter. Yes, Ross had read it. In fact, he had answered every question Zoe put to him, yet making it painfully obvious to her that all was not as it had been.

When she tried talking to Mike about it he became even more reticent, saying less than usual for even a basically quiet man. And if, as happened once or twice, she persisted, he actually buried his nose in work and said he was too busy to chatter. The third time this happened, Zoe gave him a long hard look, then quickly let herself out of his office. She wouldn't go back unless specifically invited. Mike had gone over to the opposition.

Whether Ross had made him change his mind or not she couldn't say, but the result was the same. She had lost the one ally who could have done her any good. She took this defection hard. She had needed him and he had known it. She tried to remain cheerful, but it became increasingly harder as the days went by.

She retreated into her singing as the sole means of expressing her deeper emotions. It was natural to sing the blues, and far from alienating her audience, it drew them. If it was true that misery loved company, then the major part of the audience were sharing her despair.

Then, three weeks after Ross had gone, she received a letter which sent her haring along to Mike's office in a high state of alarm. She slapped the sheet of paper on the desk before him, dislodging a small pile of files which disgorged themselves on to the floor.

'I've had a letter.'

'So I see,' Mike replied drily, sitting back in his seat.

'I've been called to New York,' she added for clarity.

He linked his fingers under his chin. 'I guessed you would be.'

Zoe stood up, affronted by his coolness and the reminder of his defection. 'You knew about it, didn't you?'

'I was told ... the company ... would be contacting you about it.'

'You could have told me, Mike. That's what friends are for.' Zoe couldn't resist the dig.

'I am your friend, Zoe, but I'm also employed by the Corporation. I was told not to say anything. Orders from the top are not to be disregarded lightly,' Mike snapped back, clearly resenting the slur. 'Was there anything else?'

Yes, there was a lot she would like to say, but she was too angry. She retrieved her letter and glanced down its contents again. 'I have to go to New York on Friday for discussions, or something. Perhaps they're going to cut my contract.' She was really only half questioning, but Mike ignored it anyway.

'The company will book you a flight. You can pick up the ticket at the airport,' Mike informed her flatly, then startled her by adding, 'Wear something pretty.'

She did a double-take. 'I beg your pardon?'

There was a strange gleam in Mike's eyes as he enlarged upon the idea. 'It never goes down well to dress as if you were going to a funeral. Wear something that'll knock their eyes out.'

Something in the way he said it stopped her automatic disagreement. For some undisclosed reason he actually wanted her to dress up for the occasion. There was more to this than he would, or could, tell her, but he was giving her advice that it might be in her interests to accept. She was totally confused.

'OK, Mike, I will,' she conceded, speaking slowly in her bewilderment. 'You think it's serious?'

'Extremely.' Mike actually grinned.

He really could be most infuriating. 'Is that all you're going to say?' she demanded in exasperation.

Mike spread his hands deprecatingly. 'My lips are sealed and my hands are tied.'

'In that condition, it's a wonder you can function at all!' She gave him the caustic parting shot which, judging by the chuckle that followed her out of the door, had no effect whatsoever.

CHAPTER TEN

ZOE arrived in New York that Friday with a lead weight in her stomach. The letter had given her no clue as to the difficulty under discussion, and the only answer she could come up with herself was that Ross wanted her gone. It had made sleep virtually impossible and rendered her appetite non-existent once more.

She had made an effort to follow Mike's suggestion, dressing in a cream-coloured lightweight suit, adding colour with an electric-blue silk blouse, and bag and shoes to match. She knew she looked good, but only a careful application of make-up had managed to hide the mauve shadows beneath her eyes and added colour to an otherwise pasty face.

The cab driver was appreciative, and he didn't seem to mind that she barely edged a word into his monologue. If she had been less worried, she might have been petrified that during the length of the journey from the airport his eyes were more often on the rear-view mirror than the road and its teeming traffic.

He turned round in his seat when they halted at some lights. 'What was that address again, lady?' When she told him, he removed his cap and scratched his head. 'I got the street but I don't place the number. Didn't they give you no name of the building, or nothin'?' A sharp hornblast from behind rudely informed him the lights had changed and gesticulating wildly out of the window, he set the cab in motion. 'I guess we can find it.'

He did, eventually, and they both sat looking up at it through the car windows.

172

'You sure you ain't made no mistake, lady? I didn't figure no court got a number.'

Zoe looked at the impressive frontage with its steep bank of steps and colonnades, and couldn't think of an adequate reply. The only coherent thought was that Mike had been right, the company were taking it seriously. She paid her fare in a daze, and accepted his help out of the cab, managing to thank him when he urged her to take care and have a nice day.

She mounted the stone steps slowly, her sense of foreboding increasing as the distance to her destination decreased. She hadn't imagined in her wildest dreams that she would be taken to court! A friendly young woman at the information desk informed her that she was expected in room 325, and a high-speed elevator whisked her up to it faster than her stomach found comfortable. The corridor was wide as a room and her footsteps echoed noisily on the marble flooring as she searched for the right door.

A muffled voice invited her to enter in answer to her knock, and Zoe found herself, not in a courtroom as she had expected, but in a large, wood-panelled office. A woman in her late forties was already walking towards her from a desk near the window, smiling and holding out her hand.

'Hello, you must be Zoe Winthrop. I'm Mrs Armstrong, the judge's PA. I hope you had no trouble finding us, we are rather tucked away up here.' She guided Zoe by the arm, still smiling, and increasing Zoe's puzzlement. What judge? 'Now I mustn't keep you. You are expected, so go straight in, and good luck.' Mrs Armstrong ushered her to a door set between loaded bookshelves and knocked softly.

Zoe was in the next room before she could draw breath. She had found her initial reception rather overwhelming and incomprehensible, but it was nothing to what she felt when she focused on the other occupants. The room seemed positively crowded until her confusion eased and she saw there were only five of them.

Marian and Mike stood to one side of the room, both of their faces wearing expressions that crossed between anxiety and delight. Marian was resplendent in a salmon-pink crêpe dress, while Mike outdid himself in a well-cut suit. She raised an eyebrow in stunned surprise.

Seated at a large desk opposite her was a complete stranger who had to be the judge, for he had that air about him. His hair was greying and so was his moustache, and he was smiling at her benevolently. Her other eyebrow shot up, and with it her bemusement began to turn into a fermenting indignation.

Close beside him stood an extremely elegant couple. She didn't know them but she could make a guess, for the man was the spitting image of Ross, minus the hard edges. He could only be his brother, which would make the woman at his side his wife. They were smiling at her too.

What were they all doing here? Why hadn't her friends told her they were to be here too? And why was it necessary for Ross's relatives to be present? Her mind buzzed without hope of finding an answer, then a movement by one of the windows drew her gaze and she quite literally swayed in shock.

It was Ross. He stood with his back to the light, a stiff, silent figure, waiting for her reaction. She couldn't have said what he was wearing for her eyes flew to his face. For a moment her heart put her anger aside and sought solace for her bruised emotions. She didn't have a clue what was happening, but just to be able to see him again was a miracle she hadn't dared hope for. He moved, and muted sunlight fell on his face. Her heart skipped in her chest and settled in a higher gear. His eyes were burning with a steady green glow and they roved her face and figure as if she were a treasure recovered after being thought lost for ever. He was smiling too, but it was strained, pulling lines at the corners of his mouth. He looked as if he hadn't been sleeping well either, and Zoe's first instinct was to go to him and ease the strain away.

It was Marian who interrupted their silent appraisal by crossing to hug her tightly. 'You had me worried. I know it's traditional to be late, but I thought you weren't coming at all.'

Zoe's mind somersaulted. Traditional? Her stunned brain assimilated the surprising fact that there was some sort of conspiracy going on, but even then she didn't see daylight. 'Late for what?' she asked in a daze.

'For our wedding,' Ross supplied softly, and all eyes turned in his direction.

A rush of heat invaded Zoe's cheeks at those three words and her heart leapt with joy. Then sanity returned. What was he trying to do to her? What hoops was he going to put her through this time?

Her eyes searched his frantically, and could find only a desperate sincerity reflected back at her. In that instant Zoe saw red. How insensitive could he be? After all these weeks, and all the things he had said, to expect her to be grateful . . . She took a step towards him, her raised hand drawing back to aim an angry slap at his cheek, but Ross caught her wrist before it made contact.

'Don't, Zoe,' he entreated, his tone agonised.

Zoe tried to wrench her hand away. 'How could you! Oh God! how could you say that? Is this some sort of perverted joke?' she demanded, seeing him wince, and hating herself for feeling pleased at getting through to him.

'Young woman,' the judge spoke up from his desk, drawing both their heads round to suffer his critical gaze, 'do you think I would involve myself in such an act?'

Zoe stared him out, and she could swear there was a twinkle in his eye. 'No, your honour,' she assured him, then turned back to Ross. 'But even a judge can be fooled.'

Ross was pale beneath his tan. 'Will you listen to me?'

The opening was there. 'Tell me why I should. Tell me why I should allow you a privilege you denied me,' she shot back bitterly.

That hurt him, but his pained gaze acknowledged she had the right to say it. Yet it didn't move him from his resolve to have his say. Keeping a firm hold of Zoe's wrist, Ross pulled her to a door in the corner, muttered a brisk, 'Excuse us,' then proceeded to bundle her unceremoniously inside what turned out to be a washroom.

Zoe turned on him immediately. 'How dare you connive to bring me here?'

Ross sighed deeply, letting her go. 'Darling, there was no other way.' He attempted to take her in his arms but she struck his hand away.

'Don't darling me! After all that you said, the disgusting things you implied about me, how could you set up this . . . this farce!' There was a wealth of hurt in every angry word.

A nerve twitched beside his mouth. 'Sit down, Zoe,' he urged, and because her legs were shaking, she sank gratefully on to the toilet seat. What he said then took her remaining strength away. 'I know my mother lied to me.'

Hastily she lowered her head, feeling faint. When the whirling sensation left her she looked up again. 'You know?'

Ross hooked a leg over the corner of the sink, letting it take his weight as he flexed his shoulders. Her eyes rested on his profile, watching the tensing movement of his jaw. When he turned to look at her there was a bleakness in his eyes.

'After you left that day, I had lunch with my parents. That was when I had the first intimation that you were telling the truth. My mother grew careless. She said some things which just didn't gel with what she had said before. She also told me things about you which you hadn't even told me. It was obvious that she had had you very thoroughly investigated. She knew when and where I'd bought that ring, when even I didn't know. You may not believe me, but I felt sick and disgusted, and there was murder in my heart. I had every intention of coming after you and begging you to forgive me, to listen to your story as you had wanted me to.'

Zoe's heart lurched at his haggard face. 'Why didn't you? Why let me go through all that?' she questioned, her anger draining away.

'Because for once in my life I was afraid. I came very close to facing them with what they had done when I realised it would be a tactical error. They had successfully removed you before and I knew they would do it again given the chance. I had to get them away from you. To make them believe I still believed what I was growing more and more certain was a parcel of lies.'

Zoe swallowed back the joy that was lightening her heart. 'That's why you went away?'

Ross combed shaky fingers through his hair. 'It was important to leave you safe on Mariposa whilst I did my own checking. I hated the idea. I wanted to see you, to tell you how much I loved you and that I was beginning to believe you. Instead I had to go. To leave without a word. It will be a long time before I can forgive them for what they did.

'How can I ever understand why they did it? I wouldn't have believed it possible if all the evidence didn't corroborate it. I thought I was going mad. I needed desperately to remember, but I couldn't. All I had to go on was the knowledge that you loved me enough to come after me. I put my trust in that. I spoke to John, as you told me to, and the staff at the hospital. I've never felt so sickened in all my life. It was worse to know that I had fallen for their lies.'

Zoe's hand went to his knee in a small comforting gesture. All the anxious months seemed suddenly never to have been. 'But darling, you didn't know enough not to.'

His hand covered hers, clenching it tightly. 'Do you know what I did after speaking to John?'

Her eyes flickered over his, her love for him glowing there. 'No.'

He swallowed and looked straight at her. 'I cried. I never cry, but I sat there and I couldn't stop.'

Zoe gasped, and in a second she was on her feet and in his arms, her hands holding tightly to the cloth of his jacket. With a groan, Ross buried his face in the sweetly scented hollow of her neck.

'All that pain and wasted time, Zoe,' he declared raggedly.

'It's over now,' she breathed into his hair, blinking back her own tears. 'We must forget it.'

'How the hell can I? I didn't even know you were hurt in the crash too. You could have died. When John told me ... I'll never forgive myself.'

Zoe pulled away enough to see him. 'That's enough,

Ross. We neither of us died and we've both healed. I don't blame you beause you couldn't remember. It was wrong for your parents to tell you lies, but it's not your fault that you believed them. You didn't know any different. If you had known, I know you would have been as concerned as you are now.' It would take some time, but they had to forget and carry on with their lives. There was no other way.

What they had to be thankful for was that, despite everything, they were going to be together again.

'It really is over, darling,' she assured him again.

Ross eased her away, framing her face with unsteady hands. There was a light of love burning fiercely from his green eyes. 'Not quite, my love. I brought you here to marry you. I love you. When I think of all the things I said to you, I shudder. Words don't seem adequate to tell you how I regret it, but I'm sorry for every one of them. I was hurt and angry, but that doesn't seem a good excuse. I should have trusted you. I . . .'

Her lips on his silenced him. 'I knew why you acted like that, even though it hurt me. But it takes more than that to kill my love for you. Don't you remember I told you I'd be waiting?' She smiled deep into his eyes, watching as a weight seemed to lift away from him.

'I held on to that like a drowning man,' he admitted.

Zoe's fingers found a lock of hair and played with it. 'Why did you go to such lengths today?'

He grinned. 'Paranoia. I won't feel safe until my ring is on your finger. Jack thought I was crazy, but then he hadn't lived through the nightmare. The thought that kept going through my head was that if they knew nothing they couldn't hurt you. Are you going to put me out of my misery? Are you going to marry me?'

There were more explanations to be sought and given, but they could wait. Everything could wait for ever. Ross loved her. Her wedding ceremony waited on the other side of the door. What else was necessary?

She gave a watery laugh. 'I'll marry you. I'm not letting you get away now.'

Laughing, they exchanged a kiss that said everything.

A collective sigh went round the judge's chambers when they emerged smiling from the washroom. The judge rose from his chair to shake her hand.

'I thought you two might have slipped down a pipe, you were so long. I'm Noah Carmody, and I'm pleased to make your acquaintance at last, Zoe. I may call you that, I hope, as an old and trusted friend of your fiancé's?' He indicated they should sit in the chairs before him. 'You forgot to say you hadn't asked the lady the pertinent question,' he charged Ross with a heavy judicial frown.

Zoe felt Ross's hand tighten on hers and he threw her a smile. 'I did ask her a long time ago, but I don't remember doing it.'

Judge Carmody didn't bat an eyelid but his gaze was shrewd. 'Sounds to me like there's a mighty interesting story here. I'd like to hear it but I have to be in court in an hour, and we do have a wedding to perform. You can invite me to dinner one evening and satisfy my curiosity.'

Zoe went through the most important occasion of her life in something close to a dream. She kept glancing at Ross from the corner of her eye to make sure he was really there, because she still found it hard to believe this was actually happening. Only when Ross slipped a heavy band of gold on to her wedding finger did it really sink in, and when he produced a ring for her to give him, she thought she might burst with happiness.

There were hugs and congratulations all round when the brief ceremony was over and the judge had taken the first opportunity of kissing the bride. Ross introduced her to Jack and his wife, Michelle. She liked them at once. They were open and honest people who welcomed her warmly. Then it was Mike's turn.

He kissed her cheek under Ross's eagle eye. 'Am I forgiven?'

Zoe gave him a look that would have daunted a brave man. 'Do you think you should be?'

Mike looked to his friend for support. 'Back me up, Ross. Tell her I was only acting under orders.'

Zoe considered her new husband carefully. He shrugged his shoulders and grinned. Later she would have more to say about this elaborate charade.

'I forgive you, Mike, now I know who to blame.'

Mike whistled. 'That doesn't sound too good for you, pal,' he said to Ross, who wasn't too upset by the implication.

'I'll take my chances.' He smiled at her confidently.

Later they returned to Ross's apartment. Zoe took to it at once. It was converted from an old brownstone building, and covered the whole of the top floor. Its welcoming warmth met her the second she stepped inside. Ross's personality was everywhere, in the comfortable furnishings, the rows of books and records, even down to the prints on the walls and the houseplants.

She discarded her jacket and Ross did the same. His tie followed it, and he released the buttons of his shirt at neck and wrist, leaving a tantalising glimpse of hair on his chest and forearms. He came up behind her and twisted her into his arms.

'Mrs Lyneham,' he stated with satisfaction, burying his lips in the soft warmth of her neck.

Her arms glided up to his shoulders. 'Till death us do part,' she vowed.

He groaned and moved away to pull her down with

him on to the couch. His lips sought hers, parting them
with a passion that made her sigh and return it with
interest. Yet she didn't fail to sense there was something
else in the heated plundering of her lips and the hands
that held her tightly to him. When he let her go, she
looked at him enquiringly. He took her hands between
his, playing with her rings—the one he had put there less
than an hour ago, and the one he didn't remember.
Unconsciously his hand began to run up and down her
silk-covered arm, and Zoe was aware of the return of
tension in his long frame. She stiffened too, looking into
his pensive face, knowing he had to tell her something
that was hurting him.

'God, Zoe, I wish I didn't have to say this, but I must
be completely honest with you, as I believe you've
always tried to be with me. I've read your letter and
talked to John. I know that we met and fell in love on
Crete and were going to be married.' He paused, easing
away to frame her face with his hand, staring searching-
ly into her golden eyes. 'I still don't remember any of it,
Zoe. There was no sudden headache or flash of blinding
light. I don't remember loving you.'

Zoe could feel his pain. Once it would have hurt her
too, but it wasn't necessary. She had to convince him of
that. 'Oh darling, it doesn't matter, truly it doesn't. I
came to find you because I loved you, and I hoped that
deep inside you was a love for me that was just as strong.
A love that I could win again. We found it, together. It
doesn't matter that you don't recall that other time. For
us, this is the first time.' She raised her hand to run it
softly over the taut skin of his cheek, trying, hoping, to
ease away this unwanted sorrow.

'I think you should know John believes it entirely
possible I will never remember,' he continued. 'The
accident was responsible for those lost weeks, not some

unknown trauma. It was just the luck of the gods that that length of time was lost to me. It could just as easily have been a day or a year.'

'Darling, if anything, the fact that you love me is more important because you can't remember. It means you trust me. That you know I'll never let you down.' She felt him relax and knew that at last she had convinced him.

Ross turned his head until his lips were resting in the palm of her hand. Tenderly he kissed the delicate skin, allowing the tip of his tongue to draw lazy, exciting patterns and steal her breath away.

If love had a colour, then for Zoe it was green—the emerald blaze of his eyes that bored into hers when he looked at her again.

'I wish we could have cried together, too.' His voice came low and thick to her ears, reminding her of that day on the beach. 'I hurt you and I didn't even know it. You were alone when I should have been there to help you. When we met again I told you I would try not to hurt you, and then I accused you of all those crazy things. I should have trusted you.'

Zoe watched, her face serious. 'Trusting isn't always easy. You just lost sight of it for an hour or two, that's all.'

Ross's head came a little closer until she could feel his warm breath on her cheek, and see the rapid movement of his throat. His voice was so deep and husky when he spoke that she had to strain to hear it over her own heartbeats. 'You deserve so much for keeping faith, for not giving up on me. What can I promise you? What do you want from me, darling?'

Zoe lowered her lashes to hide the possessive gleam she knew she must show in her eyes as she considered her answer. Then she spoke the simple truth. 'I want everything. I want the man who loves me, and laughs with me. I want your children, so that we can love them together. You see, I really don't ask for much. I want you, as you are,' she whispered, delivering her words almost as a vow. She asked him for all the things that cost nothing but love and had a price beyond measure.

His gaze burned into her. 'Oh God! How I love you,' he breathed painfully as his lips closed on hers, showing her, more clearly than he could say, just how much she meant to him.

There was so much they still had to say to each other, but this was not the time for it. Now they needed to express their love in the turbulent glory of passion. With tender eagerness Ross removed her clothes and then his own, and among the soft cushions of the couch, he worshipped her body and enslaved her soul. The only sounds to disturb the cocooning silence were stifled gasps and moans of pleasure as they took each other out beyond the realms of their conscious minds, to a plateau where for one brief moment in time they shared the tumultuous flames of ecstasy.

Later they lay in a breathless tangle of golden limbs. Ross's hand lazily caressed the velvet curve of her hip and the other rested possessively on her breast. Zoe's head lay cushioned on his chest, while her hands idly stroked the dampness from his body. Contentment weaved its misty threads around her. The solid strength in the gentle rise and fall of his chest was all the security she needed.

She felt Ross sigh heavily.

'Was I truly your first lover?'

Zoe knew these were the questions he had to ask, to know through her the moments that were precious to her but which he might never remember. She pressed a row of tiny kisses along the base of his throat. 'Yes.'

Unknowingly his hand closed tightly around her hip. 'And was it good for you, that first time?'

Zoe raised her head to look at him through heavy-lidded eyes. His eyes were misty and his jaw was rigid with tension, and she raised her hand to run it along the stern lines. 'You were gentle and patient. You brought me to life, made me aware of how wonderful it is to be a woman.' She saw him open his mouth to say more, and guessing what it might be, she raised herself to stop him with a kiss. 'No, yes and maybe.'

With relief she saw she had destroyed his sober mood. His teeth flashed as he grinned down at her. 'Think you're clever, don't you? I bet you think you know what I was going to say.'

She grinned back, nodding. 'Um-hm. No, you didn't hurt me. Yes, you enjoyed it too. And . . .' she cast him a very provocative look from under her lashes, 'and maybe I'll tell you what we did . . . later.'

Laughter rumbled through his chest, bouncing her about. 'OK, so you did know. You aren't going to let me brood, are you?'

'I absolutely refuse to. The only difference between then and now is that I had never made love before. Since then you've been benefiting from your own teaching, and if it isn't up to your expectation, then you only have yourself to blame.'

'You little devil!' Ross was galvanised into action by the implication of her words. The tussle was bravely engaged and very noisy, only ending when they inadvertently rolled off the couch and landed heavily on the floor.

Already winded, Ross stole what remaining breath Zoe possessed by closing his mouth on hers and kissing her long and hard. Having reduced her to abject slavery, he loomed over her, grinning triumphantly.

'I do believe I love you, Mrs Lyneham.'

'Mr and Mrs Ross Lyneham. I like the sound of that. Your parents won't though.' Zoe reminded him of the only dark spot on their horizon.

Ross didn't look worried. In fact, if anything, he smiled more broadly. 'I refuse to let them spoil today. We'll face them with the truth in a few days, but now we're married there's not a thing they can do.'

If he could be confident about it, so could she, Zoe decided, though not without a qualm. Her relationship with Cole and Deirdre would never be easy, but she would do her best for Ross's sake. She held him close to her, as if by sheer effort of will she could ward off all devils.

Ross raised himself on his elbows and ran a finger tenderly over her lips. 'So defensive, ready to fight for me again. Your mother said you would.' He saw her surprise and nodded. 'Yes, I've met them. I flew to London to tell them I intended marrying you. I liked them very much. I promised to take you to see them as soon as possible.'

'Why didn't you tell me before?' she yelped accusingly.

'Because,' he drawled, 'I was busy doing other things. Things you didn't seem averse to, I might add.' He emphasised the point by running a hand experimentally down to her hip and up again to fasten on her breast. His teasing fingers sent a ripple of pleasure through her system and set her heart thumping with expectancy.

'Cad!'

His eyes crinkled as he laughed. 'I can stop if you don't like it.'

'Don't you dare!' she squeaked, dropping her own hand to hold his where it was.

'You'd better make up your mind whether I stop or

go, or I might make it up for you,' Ross threatened, shifting his strong body until he lay between her parted thighs. He moved against her suggestively, and Zoe gasped as a wave of pleasure burst its way upwards. 'Well?' he asked again, lowering his lips to the now frantically beating pulse at the base of her throat.

Zoe closed her eyes, striving to keep her senses from being swamped by the havoc he was creating. 'Don't we have to meet the others for dinner soon?' she gulped, shuddering as his mouth forayed up to her ear.

'They'll wait,' he murmured, drawing her lobe between his lips, growling in satisfaction when she started to move beneath him.

Zoe gave in. Sliding her hand into the thickness of his hair, she tugged his head up until she could see his face. His eyes were hot and slumbrous, and a flush stained his cheeks. She could feel the heat of her own cheeks and knew her eyes were sending out messages he had no difficulty reading: I love you, I want you.

'I adore you,' he breathed unsteadily. 'Thank you for not giving up on me.'

'You're entirely welcome,' she teased, and received him into her embrace. She had found peace at last. She had come home.

Coming in April
Harlequin Category Romance Specials!

Look for six new and exciting titles from this mix of two genres.

4 Regencies—lighthearted romances set in England's Regency period (1811-1820)

2 Gothics—romance plus suspense, drama and adventure

Regencies

Daughters Four by Dixie Lee McKeone
She set out to matchmake for her sister, but reckoned without the Earl of Beresford's devilish sense of humor.

Contrary Lovers by Clarice Peters
A secret marriage contract bound her to the most interfering man she'd ever met!

Miss Dalrymple's Virtue by Margaret Westhaven
She needed a wealthy patron—and set out to buy one with the only thing she had of value....

The Parson's Pleasure by Patricia Wynn
Fate was cruel, showing her the ideal man, then making it impossible for her to have him....

Gothics

Shadow over Bright Star by Irene M. Pascoe
Did he want her shares to the silver mine, her love—or her life?

Secret at Orient Point by Patricia Werner
They seemed destined for tragedy despite the attraction between them....

The passionate saga
that began with SARAH continues in the compelling,
unforgettable story of

Elizabeth

MAURA SEGER

In the aftermath of the Civil War, a divided nation—and two
tempestuous hearts—struggle to become one.

Harlequin Intrigue
Adopts a New Cover Story!

We are proud to present to you
the new Harlequin Intrigue cover design.

Look for two exciting new stories each month, which mix a contemporary, sophisticated romance with the surprising twists and turns of a puzzler . . . romance with "something more."

ATTRACTIVE, SPACE SAVING BOOK RACK

Display your most prized novels on this handsome and sturdy book rack. The hand-rubbed walnut finish will blend into your library decor with quiet elegance, providing a practical organizer for your favorite hard-or soft-covered books.

Only $9.95

Approximately 16" x 8" when assembled

Assembles in seconds!

To order, rush your name, address and zip code, along with a check or money order for $10.70* ($9.95 plus 75¢ postage and handling) payable to *Harlequin Reader Service*:

Harlequin Reader Service
Book Rack Offer
901 Fuhrmann Blvd.
P.O. Box 1396
Buffalo, NY 14269-1396

Offer not available in Canada.

*New York and Iowa residents add appropriate sales tax.

BKR-1A

CAROLE MORTIMER

JUST ONE NIGHT

Hawk Sinclair—Texas millionaire and owner of the exclusive
Sinclair hotels, determined to protect his son's inheritance.
Leonie Spencer—desperate to protect her sister's happiness.

They were together for just one night.
The night their daughter was conceived.

Blackmail, kidnapping and attempted murder add suspense
to passion in this exciting bestseller.

The success story of Carole Mortimer continues with *Just
One Night*, a captivating romance from the author of the
bestselling novels, *Gypsy* and *Merlyn's Magic*.

**Available in March
wherever paperbacks are sold.**